JOURNEY TO ICELAND

Also by Ron Briggs

Yellow Hair Series

Erik Haraldsson

Tor's Saga

Cass

Westward

JOURNEY TO ICELAND

YELLOW HAIR
BOOK FIVE

RON BRIGGS

WOLFPACK
PUBLISHING
— EST 2019 —

FOREWORD

This is a work of fiction. The characters, events, and places are created by the author. An honest attempt has been made to describe real cultures and interactions as they may have taken place early in the eleventh century AD.

The cultures depicted as interacting in this story are the Norwegian Norse, Greenlandic Norse, Icelandic Norse, Mahican, Dorset Culture, riverine Lenni Lenape, Micmac, Mississippian, Mononga-hela Phase, Late Fort Ancient, Illini, and Owasco or proto-Iroquois (also called Haudenosaunee by some). The author hopes the reader finds the depictions of the cultures and physical descrip-tions of the places found in this book to be accurate.

The descriptions reflect the transition from Middle Woodland to Late Woodland North American traditions and touches on the blossoming of the Mississippian culture that would have a great influence over the next several generations.

There are references that indicate it was illegal for a Norseman to marry and/or have children with a "Skræling," a derogatory name used by the Norse to describe indigenous peoples encountered west of Iceland, in both Greenland and Iceland. I could not find any examples or punishments handed out in any reference.

This fifth book of the saga deals with Tor and Bright Moon making their way across northeastern Turtle Island (North America to the modern world) and finding a way to Norse colonies in Greenland and, finally, Iceland. Their epic journey is fraught with danger, accomplishment, prejudice, and sorrow. But strength of character brings them to the place where their (fictional) legacy lives on.

A study published in 2010 indicated a small population of modern Icelanders have a mitochondrial DNA marker indicating a female ancestor from indigenous populations of North Americans dating to about 1000 to 1050 AD. This story has Heidi (a.k.a. Bright Moon, Cass, and Heidr Tungl) arriving in Iceland around 1030 AD. The story presented is not a historical document, but the author desires the reader finds the saga both possible and plausible.

JOURNEY TO ICELAND

CHAPTER I
GOODBYE

"You have shared my sleeping skins for more than a half-moon, now. Are you sure you do not want to go with Yellow Hair to the far north wilds to find his people?" Corn Stalk asked Traveler as they lay awake, waiting for the shortest day of the year to begin.

"My place is now at your side, wife. I am content here. But do not push too hard, or I may think you are bored with me," Traveler teased with a grin on his face she could not see in the darkness.

Her hand on his manhood told him she was not bored. After they finished, they were out of the longhouse and down on the partially frozen river to meet the winter solstice sunrise. Most of Monongahela Village was there to greet the sun and pray for a short, mild winter. Despite their

1

prayers, they were prepared for a long, hard winter. The corn harvest had been very good, and they had an adequate supply stored in corn cribs throughout the village. Each lodge also had good supplies of dried venison and turkey, along with dried berries, nuts, fruit, roots, and leaves. The long nights of storytelling would be comfortable for at least three more moons. By then, the people would be ready for the Awakening Moon and to move about outside the village palisade.

Traveler, Yellow Hair, Bright Moon, and Long Cat spent much of their time planning the trip to Sun Town and up the Lenape River into the unknown, even though Traveler would not be going on this adventure. Red Oak joined them often and finally decided that he would bring a squad of warriors to go along to escort Long Cat's party to Sun Town. His party would be of use if they ran into trouble, and he would explore some country he had never seen. Corn Stalk, of course, objected to him going so far from home, but he was a grown man and could make his own decisions. Red Oak was a natural leader and had no trouble recruiting five warriors to accompany him. He promised to bring back a canoe filled with trade goods.

As the winter progressed, Bright Moon's belly grew along with the glow in her eyes. She looked forward to bringing Yellow Hair's son into the world. Corn Stalk's apprehension and melancholy grew with Bright Moon's belly. The thought of losing the woman she considered her granddaughter along with her baby was a burden Corn Stalk hated to bear. "Powers beyond our vision control their lives," Traveler often told her in an effort to comfort her. His consolation did little to make her feel better about the arrival of spring.

"Should you not at least wait until the child comes before setting out on such a strenuous journey?" Corn Stalk asked Bright Moon one day when the men were all out hunting on snowshoes.

"Grandmother, I know you long to know this little one." Bright Moon placed her hand on her growing abdomen. "But Long Cat's words are true when he advises us to get to this faraway land as soon as we can. There is no promise that a great canoe will be there as it is. The journey will take us more than a sun cycle, so we really must go as soon as we can. The child should come while we are in Sun Town, where the people love Yellow Hair. I will send word with some trader that the birth went well, and we are all healthy and strong. I ask not that you be happy that we are leaving but smile that we are together and on our way to make my husband's life whole again. I think that is the reason the gods brought us together."

Corn Stalk hugged Bright Moon while she shed a tear down the young woman's back. "If there is no great canoe to greet you, a place in this village will always be waiting for you."

By the spring equinox, most of the snow had left the valley, and the rivers ran free of ice. The higher hills and north-facing slopes still had deep snows that would soon be melting and making river travel treacherous, so the small group heading east patiently waited for the Planting Moon. Packs were loaded with trade goods, and new traveling clothes were made. Corn Stalk helped Bright Moon make a dress that would accommodate her expanding girth.

"You need her more than I do." Traveler lovingly painted a new coat of pitch over the seams and skin of his bark canoe. "Promise you will take good care of her. That is all I ask." He kept his eyes on the upturned canoe, avoiding eye contact with Yellow Hair.

"I feel wrong going upriver in this canoe without you. We have seen a lot in a few sun cycles, you and me. I will surely miss your company." Yellow Hair choked on his words.

"Now do not go getting sentimental on me—this is hard enough as it is. You need to follow your destiny, and my place is here. I have finally grown up and accepted responsibility. Don't make me wish I had made another decision." Traveler looked into the gray, early spring sky. "And make good trades for all those Cahokian beads and gorgets. The women of Sun Town love them."

"I have no way to pay you for all those goods. You should keep them to make Long Cat honest when he returns." Yellow Hair's attempted humor fell short of his intention. The mood grew more somber.

"Long Cat will not make the trek over the mountains again. He is older than I am. He only came west to show you that thick cloth hat and to make a bit of profit. Once he gets you to Round Track Village and returns to Lenape Town, I think he will find a woman to settle in with. He is tired. I have seen it before—I feel it. A man just runs out of travel blood. And you will need everything I have given you, and more, to make it to your people. I hope this canoe makes it all the way for you."

"It will—it was crafted with Norse hands!"

"Yes, and Real People hands, too! Maybe one day you can bring your people here and show us how to work the metal so we can make our own great winged canoes."

"I am not sure you want my people here, Traveler. My people have their own ways and very little patience with others."

"You have fit in here pretty well. Are you not

happy? Is Bright Moon not enough for you? Or are you different, somehow, from your clans?" It dawned on him that they had never really talked deeply about what Yellow Hair's people were like.

"I am perfectly happy with her. God could not have found a more perfect angel to fulfill my life. However, most Norsemen are more rigid than me, I think. I heard nothing but scorn and disrespect for the people of Vinland and Markland from the sailors who had run into them. My father was different. His experience with the boy, Peluk, had changed his opinion of the Skræling. And he taught me to respect any I ran into. Little did I know I would end up in this world—completely foreign to anything I had ever known. But my father was an exception. I do not think most would get along with the people here. They would be most interested in the yellow metal and the shiny silver metal in Cahokia, maybe some of the skins. The rest they might see as beneath them, if you understand what I mean."

"Do you think it wise to bring Bright Moon among these people? It sounds like it might be dangerous for her."

"My family is highly respected. No one would bring harm to any of us. But Bright Moon does look different—I will need to stay close until everyone learns who she is."

"You know more of that than I do." Traveler picked up his tools and set the steaming pitch bag away from the fire so it would harden until needed again. He looked longingly at the canoe again. "I think that will do."

Corn Stalk stood next to Traveler at the canoe landing as the four travelers and their warrior escort prepared to leave. Her grandson, Red Oak, and five warriors would accompany them to the Sun Town. Blue Deer had grown powerful and would help Long Cat paddle his long dugout trader's canoe. Bright Moon and Yellow Hair would take the birch bark canoe that Yellow Hair helped Traveler build three winters past before they made their way to Cahokia.

Corn Stalk looked on in disbelief as Bright Moon gracefully moved about, packing baskets and bundles into the canoe. She displayed none of the clumsiness usually associated with a woman in her sixth moon of pregnancy. *How does she do it? Did I move like that when I carried Bear Cub, Silk, Watercress, or Poult? They are all grown now and have adult names, mates, and children of their own! Where has the time gone? Bright Moon has become quite the woman. I hope this journey does not destroy her. Nothing else has, and she has been through so much more than should be required of anyone...and to be so young!*

Corn Stalk locked her arm around Traveler's elbow. "It is like watching your own children leave home. When One Bear joined with his wife and went to live with Deer Clan, it seemed he was moving across the world. It was only three longhouses distant. Now, watching these children prepare to leave forever is like a piece of my heart is ripping away and going with them."

"I never thought I would become attached to any human being. But those two taught me that two hearts beating together can be stronger than a whole tribe of warriors or all the gods of Cahokia." He squeezed her arm. "I will miss them both, but I know they are perfectly suited to take care of themselves. I pity anyone who gets in their way. Red Oak will return by the Hunter's Moon and give us a full report. Maybe he will be there when the baby arrives."

CHAPTER 2

JUNIATA RIVER

Bright Moon was relieved when they were finally able to float their canoes in a river flowing east. The portage over the high hills wore on her more than anything she had done up to that time. *Child, you are wearing me down,* she thought as she heaved to catch her breath and stretch her tired back and leg muscles, her hand resting on her swollen belly. Yellow Hair noticed her stress and declared they would rest a bit before starting downriver. In a finger of time, they were drinking fresh tea and munching on venison jerky.

About mid-morning a handful of days later, they pulled into a canoe landing by a small cluster of lodges. Yellow Hair counted ten-and-two people standing on the bank as they slid to a stop. His open hands, palms up gesture was met with friendly greetings. He noted one young man was dressed differently than the others. A dugout larger than the other two canoes and loaded with bundles of skins and trader bags also did not escape Yellow Hair's notice.

"Sorry," the young man said, shrugging his shoulders. "I think I traded for all of their goods. My name is Red Fin, I am a trader in these lands. Your reputation precedes you. We have all heard of the yellow hair. Some of your dress I think comes from far to the west. Where would you be going on this river?"

"Are you the chief of this village? Is that why you ask questions to strangers?" Yellow Hair turned to the oldest woman in the group. "I am Yellow Hair, once an adopted son of the Turtle Clan in Sun Town. My companions are my wife, Bright Moon, formerly a maiden of the Water Plant Clan of Long Pine Village, Long Cat and Blue Deer, traders from Lenape Town on the Lenape River, and Red Oak, warrior of the Corn Clan of Monongahela Village. The five warriors are with Red Oak. We are traveling to Sun Town where my wife will give birth to her first child."

"I am Moss, mother of Bobcat, head man of our family. We are of no clan or village. We make our living by hunting and fishing in these lands as well as growing a few squashes and beans. Our harvest has been good so far this spring, and our meat caches are full. Your woman looks as if she could use a rest. You have more than a moon of hard traveling to reach Sun Town. I have to wonder if the child will wait that long. You are welcome to stay here for a few days. Red Fin was preparing to leave when you came down the river. There is an empty lodge you can use."

Moss had a friendly, welcoming expression on her face. Her tongue was Lenape with a slightly different dialect, but Yellow Hair was able to converse smoothly with her. Yellow Hair and Long Cat had been teaching Bright Moon and Red Oak the tongue since they left Monongahela Village so they could understand most of what was being said.

"I think I might want to stay and hear what Yellow Hair has to say. He must have some interesting stories, and could this be Cass, infamous killer of men?" Red Fin gestured to Bright Moon confidently.

"I am giving the extra lodge to these travelers, and you are packed. Be on your way, your welcome here has expired," Bobcat replied sternly, turning to face Red Fin squarely.

"All right, but you will welcome me back after harvest when I bring you a canoe full of corn."

Then Red Fin climbed into his canoe and shoved off downriver.

Yellow Hair noticed he was moving faster than necessary. *Is he angry at being asked to leave, or is there something else?* he pondered.

Long Cat spoke to Bobcat. "He seems rather uncouth for a trader. Where is he from? I have never seen him before."

"He has been coming around every other moon, even through the winter for more than a sun cycle now. He never says where he is from, but always seems to have things we want. Honestly, I do not trust him, but he has not yet cheated us. Maybe it is just his brash personality."

"Does he go upriver from here? There are several families like yours along this river."

"Usually. I was surprised he just went downriver this time. He came from downriver, so I expected him to go upriver and stop back here for more free food. He showed up here three days past and kept asking if we had seen anything, or anyone unusual coming downriver. Almost like he was expecting you." Bobcat had suspicion in his voice now.

Bright Moon whispered something in Yellow Hair's ear. He looked her in the eye questioningly and spoke up. "He is on his way to tell Ganeco that we are here. If we stay here more than overnight, we are endangering Bobcat's family. We will leave in the morning."

"Ganeco has no camp in these lands. He is busy building up the old Mud Town, which he calls Ganeco Village. He wants to gain control of the whole Mud River all the way to Blue Crab Town. So far the Blue Crab warriors have kept him away from the lower river, so I have heard. We wish to stay out of all of that. That is why we stay here. If we must, we can find a place farther upriver." Bobcat was obviously skeptical of Red Fin.

"Flint Carrier," Long Cat muttered, mostly to himself. "I saw his canoe in Squirrel Tail Village. He trades along the northern routes and is friends with the Haudenosaunee peoples. He must have told Ganeco that Yellow Hair was moving up the Spirit River."

"We will be gone long before he can send warriors here. He considers me an enemy, and I will not repay your kindness by endangering you. We should be on our way now." Yellow Hair turned to his companions for support.

"You will do no such thing! My family will feed you and give your woman a needed rest." Moss was not to be denied her offer.

As if to emphasize her ultimatum, thunderbirds sent their rumbling promise of a storm down the valley. The travelers quickly unloaded their canoes and moved everything under the cover of the lean-tos adjoining each building. Deer hides were stretched over the baskets to shed any rain that might blow in under the shelters.

And rain it did. All through the night, thunder rumbled following flashes of lightning. Long Cat guessed it must have rained a hand deep on level ground. Water filled the shallow trenches surrounding the small lodges and seeped into the door openings. It finally subsided and stopped before the sun rose the following morning.

Yellow Hair was anxious to get on the swollen river and had everyone up and ready when the morning sky showed its first graying. Bright Moon was the first to carry a soggy-bottomed skin bag full of trade goods down to the canoe landing. As she started down the steep trail, she looked back to tell Yellow Hair the bag was not too heavy for her. When she did, her foot slipped into an eroded rivulet the rain had carved into the trail. Her ankle turned, and she went down in a heap, rolling down another couple of body lengths after she hit the ground. Lightning shot through her foot and up to her knee. It was the worst physical pain she had ever felt.

Running to her aid when he saw her fall, Yellow Hair lost his footing on the slippery trail, fell, and slid down the slope and into her. She tried to laugh, but the pain in her ankle was too great to ignore. He rolled over and got up on his knees and looked at her ankle. Her mid-calf moccasin was stretched tight around the ankle joint already. It was impossible for him to determine if any bones were broken, but any kind of flexing or weight bearing was out of the question. Carefully, he cut the moccasin and fawnskin sock away. The swollen flesh was already discolored with a red "bow" running under the bone on the outside. Above that the bulging skin was almost black with yellowish fringes. There would be no traveling that day. He slipped and sloshed around until he got his balance and helped her to her feet. By then everyone was at the landing offering a hand. She made an attempt to put weight on that foot, but it was just not going to happen.

By midday two days later, she was hobbling around pretty well with a slat of bark under her foot with two more slats wrapped to the sides keeping her foot from wobbling. The whole affair was lashed together with cedar bark ropes and thick sinew strings.

At sunrise the next morning, their canoes were loaded and ready to shove off downriver. "You will reach the Mud River before nightfall two days from now. If you see Blue Crab warriors, seek their protection," Bobcat advised.

"The Blue Crab Chief thinks that they were cheated when Yellow Hair did not go there to bless their town, so we are not welcome there either. We need to get to Sun Town. I know the way, but it will be a lot of lugging for Bright Moon, here. I hope the trip is not too hard on her and the child she carries," Long Cat offered.

"Wolf is with me."

"Right now, we need to avoid Ganeco. We better be on our way." Yellow Hair had once again darkened his hair with a mixture of bear grease and charcoal. A lighter shade was applied to his face and hands. He wore a long sleeve hunting shirt even though the temperatures were warm. He could dip it in the river now and then to keep cool. Best to be as inconspicuous as possible for a while.

"Do take care of yourselves," Moss said.

"Thank you for everything, Grandmother." Bright Moon hugged the old woman one last time.

"You are a sweet child, Bright Moon. May the Creator always smile on you." Moss turned away with a single tear trickling down her wrinkled cheek.

CHAPTER 3

BATTLE WITH GANECO

They followed the river all day and met no one. Just before looking for a place to put in for the night, they passed by a steep, eroded bank about three man-heights high along an outside bend on the north side of the river. Thick brush and tall trees rose above the bank. *Perfect ambush place*, Yellow Hair thought to himself. He remembered that just a little way upriver from the cliff was a small creek channel coming in from the north and perfectly screened from the east. He motioned for them to turn around and led them into the creek channel where they hid the canoes from the river.

"We will scatter along that cut bank where we turned around and cold camp tonight. I have a hunch we will have unwelcome company tomorrow. If Ganeco is who I think he is, he will have found out we were with that hermit family on this river and will be charging after us. Sorry I got you all into this mess."

"This is no mess. Ganeco and all his Minquas friends are worm testicles who need to be cut down," Long Cat said, with hate in his voice.

"No telling how many of them there will be, but I think that cut bank gives us a good ambush point. I will take the position farthest upriver and before dawn will start a campfire close to the river where we will set up a tent. They will see the fire and paddle close to that bank thinking they are sneaking up on us while we are cooking our break-fast—if they are coming and if they fall for my trick." Yellow Hair spoke with less than full confi-dence. "If they come, our object will be to wound as many as we can. Try not to kill anyone. If they are just wounded, some of the others will need to care for the wounded. Hopefully they will retreat back to Mu...Ganeco Village. We should have enough time to get to Sun Town before a war party comes after us. If Sun Town scouts discover us first, they will have a nasty surprise for any war party chasing us."

"You have a lot of 'ifs' in your plan, Yellow Hair. Perhaps we should take our chances with the Blue

Crab werowance." Long Cat did not sound very confident either.

"I will let you all decide, then, which way we go once we shed ourselves of Ganeco. But my feeling is that I would rather go somewhere I know I am welcome. Painted Turtle definitely has the strength to stop Ganeco's men."

"I go where my husband goes."

"And I go where my cousin goes." Red Oak drifted his eyes to each member of the group. His five warriors nodded their agreement.

"I never had much use for Blue Crab Village anyway." Long Cat nodded to everyone.

"All right, let's set up a lean-to here just in the brush from the river and prepare a fire pit. We will set a pot of gruel next to it so if the wind drifts downriver, they will smell it and come after us here. Perhaps their guard will be down a little if they think they caught us unawares." Yellow Hair sounded as if he could see the battle unfold.

"And if they do not come in the morning?"

"We wait. They will be along soon enough."

"Ganeco will be here." Bright Moon looked downriver as if she was experiencing a vision.

Yellow Hair looked at her, thinking she must have had one of her unexplained insights. He did not question her.

Long Cat fingered his chin for several heart-beats. "This Ganeco. He sounds like the kind of man who cannot abide someone getting the better of him. It would matter not if it has been twenty sun cycles. He is coming. And maybe you should kill him, Yellow Hair. Left alive, he will seek vengeance, whether he can find you or not, someone will pay for this little ambush of yours. I know I am staying on the Lenape River when this is over."

"Perhaps you are right, but I want him to command them back up the Mud River. If he is dead, his second might hang around fighting until we are dead, or he is. I want them away from here so we can get Bright Moon to someplace comfortable before the child comes. I hope that Ganeco can see that we have a very defendable position and attacking us would be too costly for him."

"Yes...well, you hope a lot."

Before the sun set they had their positions set and were ready for a war party coming up the Juniata River. They were less than a day from where it joined the Mud River. Coming down river from Ganeco Village was less than three days and nights. Red Fin had left Moss's campsite ten days prior.

Before color started to edge its way into the starry night, Yellow Hair had a small fire going and was warming the gruel 'bait.' His fire was smokier than normal. His luck held and the wind would carry the strong scent of burning cherrywood down the river valley. He hurried back to his position on the edge of the cut bank where his people could ambush the war party he expected.

Ganeco did not disappoint. Just after the sunrise, six canoes rounded the bend to the south. This stretch of the river flowed due south before making more bends and joining the Mud River half a day to the southeast. As they approached, Red Oak was the first to see that they wore red and black face paint—this was no trading expedition. Each canoe had a leader in front who held a strung bow with a nocked arrow and four paddlers.

They were to wait until Yellow Hair shot his arrow into the lead canoe, then they would all fire on the rest, wounding as many as they could until the canoes got out of range. Yellow Hair's plan was to wound at least two in each canoe.

As the canoes passed a bulge to the west in the south flowing river, the tendril of smoke rising from the campfire became visible. Ganeco, dressed in a red war shirt, face painted half red, half black, and a long, braided roach emanating from the back of his head was in the lead canoe and saw the smoke first. He looked at the riverbanks and signaled them to hug the east bank as they stalked their quarry.

Along the cut bank there was no place to pull a canoe ashore, so they would have to scramble across the river once the arrows started raining down. Yellow Hair made sure each member of his party had two quivers full of arrows.

When Ganeco's canoe was right in front of him, the sun broke over the hill pouring light into the canoes as they drifted along the cutbank. Yellow Hair's first arrow slammed into Ganeco's muscular left thigh. The chert-tipped arrow sliced through muscle and pinned the luckless war chief's leg to the dugout's hull. Ganeco twisted to see where the arrow came from and was blinded by the sun just as a second arrow drove into the leg of the man just behind him.

In turn, Bright Moon, Long Cat, Blue Deer, Red Oak, and five more warriors loosed their arrows with the same devastating effect. Within seconds, the six canoes were beating a hasty retreat across the river. By the time they cleared bowshot range, ten and six of the three tens of warriors were wounded in a leg or arm. Another had an arrow just below his shoulder that protruded through his chest. Hissing noises and pink blood indicated the arrow had clipped the man's lung.

Ganeco knew he was beaten. Most of their wounds were not life threatening unless they did not tend to them properly and quickly. And the best place to do that was Ganeco Village, four days away up the Mud River. *This Yellow Hair is barely more than a boy. And now he has outwitted me twice. He will not elude me again!* "Fox Tracker! Get everyone organized to get us back to Ganeco Village as quickly as possible. We need to get these men tended to."

"But Chief, there are more of us than them. We still have ten and three healthy warriors. We can cut them down like field mice fleeing a grass fire."

"Yes, and by the time you do, you will have lost more men, and those of us with wounds will have had evil spirits invade our cuts, and you'll lose more of us. Get us back to Ganeco Village so we can get healed. Then we will organize a war walk and put an end to Yellow Hair once and for all." Ganeco's painful winces made his orders almost incoherent. He had lost a lot of blood before they could get his wound to stop flowing, and he was feeling dizzy. By midafternoon all four canoes were moving back down the Juniata River toward the Mud River. It would take them four long days of hard paddling to get back to Ganeco Village, but they had no friends between the Juniata River and Ganeco Village.

Yellow Hair and his party set out at first light the next morning. They had stayed in place above the bank hidden in the trees and brush until

Ganeco's canoes rounded the bend to the south before packing back to their canoes. Red Oak and three of his men stayed above the bank to keep an eye on the river. After dark, the men rotated guard duty all night to ensure that Ganeco did not double back. While Yellow Hair was on duty, Long Cat and Red Oak marveled at how Yellow Hair had guessed exactly what Ganeco would do and had perfectly executed the plan to repel the war chief.

Bright Moon just smiled. "This is why he is my husband." Her wide smile visible in the dim light.

Before midday they reached the Mud River and followed it downstream. They were confronted at the Village of Paxtang, a Lenape settlement aligned with Blue Crab Town. Yellow Hair convinced the warriors that tried to detain them that they were to deliver this matron's daughter of Sun Town before her child was born. In the end, Long Cat traded them a bundle of beaver pelts, and Yellow Hair threw in some fine Cahokian tobacco for letting them pass through to a creek that led them northeast.

For the next moon or longer, they would have some difficult upstream paddling, strenuous walks carrying their belongings, and steep downhill trails to contend with. After a tortuous moon on the hard trails, they finally reached the Stone River and could float the final two days to Sun Town.

Bright Moon was never happier that Red Oak and his warriors were there to help them on those strenuous climbs and treacherous portages. Red Oak's men would not allow the beautiful and pregnant woman to hold up her end of a canoe with heavy packs strapped to her. Bright Moon's ankle had healed enough to put a moccasin on, but she required frequent rests. Her limp added to the help from everyone in their party. They all wanted to help the woman who had proven she could do as much work as any of them.

CHAPTER 4
SUN TOWN

Four Canoes, one led by Strong Wing, swung into the current to escort them into Sun Town even before Yellow Hair spotted the smoke from cooking fires rising above the trees.

"This woman does not resemble the last person I saw you traveling with in this canoe, Tu… Yellow Hair. I thought it was his." Strong Wing tried to sound gruff and authoritative.

"You will not make war chief if you cannot sound meaner than a baby fox." Yellow Hair could hardly believe he was here, bantering with the first friend he had in this land. They brought the canoes together and almost turned both over hugging and patting each other on the back.

"Strong Wing, Great Warrior of the Turtle

Clan, I want you to meet Bright Moon, maiden of Water Plant Clan, Long Pine Village, and wife of Yellow Hair and about to deliver his first child. In the other canoes are Red Oak, Warrior of the Corn Clan of Monongahela Village and his five Monongahela warriors. I think you already know Long Cat, Trader from Lenape Town. He has Blue Deer of the Deer Clan of Lenape Village. I will tell the stories in Matron Painted Turtle's longhouse later if we are invited. My heart sings to look upon your face, my brother." Yellow Hair was about out of breath from the long speech.

"Your transgressions have not banned you from Painted Turtle's longhouse yet, brother. And bringing this beautiful wife into the family will only increase your standing, I believe."

"We have much to tell. Let me say that we are happy to be over those last passes and on to rivers we can float! And what of you? How are things in these lands?"

"Looks like another big corn crop, and meat is plentiful. We should have a comfortable winter. But you will find a surprise or two around here." Strong Wing looked ahead as they rounded the last bend, and Sun Town's double palisade came into view. Yellow Hair reviewed for Bright Moon how he and Strong Wing were brothers and why Strong Wing was in Sun Town rather than Willet Village.

The corn leaves were bending downward and losing their deep green color, some of the ears were full, the silk turning brown. Many of the grasses and wild plants were changing to their fall colors, but the trees were just beginning to lose their full green luster. Young boys, girls, and young women could be seen in the forest in places collecting fallen nuts and acorns. Some of the boys and a few brave girls were up in trees knocking nuts to the others waiting below them.

When they slid into the canoe landing, Painted Turtle was standing at the top of the landing slope. To her right were Round Shell and Willow Branch, who was showing her third pregnancy. To her left stood Wolf Chaser, War Chief of Sun Town. He stood in a position normally reserved for the husband of the Sakimaxkwe.

Yellow Hair helped Bright Moon climb out of the canoe and up the slope to the flat area above the canoe landing. She moved as gracefully as she could with a full-term pregnancy and still nursing a sprained ankle. Yellow Hair introduced everyone in his party and was shocked to hear that Painted Turtle was married to Wolf Chaser. He had been out hunting when his lodge caught fire in the middle of the night. His two wives, three daughters, a young son, two sons-in-law, and three grandchildren, were all killed in the blaze. No one knew how the fire had started. All were asleep, and only his son escaped, but he died of his severe burns a few days later.

Painted Turtle invited the whole group under her sunshade for tea and corncakes. The day was too warm to sit in the stuffy longhouse. Yellow Hair's stories of the past sun cycle had everyone in awe. Wolf Chaser's body language said he was very skeptical of Bright Moon's history, even though her exploits on the Spirit Water River were legendary, even in Sun Town. Before Yellow Hair was finished with his stories, the sun set, and they all moved into the longhouse to get away from the mosquitoes.

While they ate a tasty venison stew, Yellow Hair told everything in chronological order up to the point where Long Cat showed up in Cahokia. Long Cat then detailed how he came to possess the wool hat which he took out and showed to Painted Turtle and Wolf Chaser. Painted Turtle was very interested in how the cloth was made and colored. Yellow Hair's memory was a bit sketchy on the details, but he got the general ideas across.

"And you think you can just wander off into this mysterious frozen northland and find your grandfather as easily finding an acorn under an oak tree?" Painted Turtle asked skeptically.

"Sakimaxkwe, nothing in our lives has come

easily so far. No, I do not think it will be easy. And we may yet have battles to fight. There is no guarantee that all of the peoples we encounter will be friendly. But we are called upon to try. I cannot be sure we will be successful."

"You would risk the lives of your beautiful wife and baby on such a dangerous adventure? Your thinking eludes me. You could have a comfortable life right here. Raise your children, be a great hunter and a part of our society."

"Grandmother, most of my life has been unexplainable. After all these sun cycles, I may not even be welcome in grandfather's lodge, but I must try. I must find out." Among the Lenape, any elder male relative was referred to as 'grandfather.' Bright Moon put her arm around him and laid her head on his shoulder.

Painted Turtle looked hard at Bright Moon. Her face showed the fatigue of the long journey that led them to her lodge. But there was also an inner strength that told her that the young woman was ready to meet any challenge set before her.

To Yellow Hair's amazement, Round Shell was cordial to him and Bright Moon. *It is apparent that my adopted sister no longer sees me as a threat.*

Willow Branch and Bright Moon detached and compared pregnancy stories while Wolf Chaser, Long Cat, and Red Oak talked about what lies ahead for the travelers. Wolf Chaser said a trader going to the west was in Sun Town and that Red Oak's party could probably follow his canoe back to Monongahela Village right after the *Gamwing* and Harvest Celebrations.

Yellow Hair and Painted Turtle were left talking to each other alone for the first time. "Tell me, Yellow Hair, what has become of Traveler? I see you using the canoe you helped him build, and I recognize his trader bags. Has something dreadful befallen him?"

"No, Grandmother, in fact he was alive and well when we left Monongahela Village. It was strange. Bright Moon told me he had chosen to settle down with her grandmother, the Head Matron of Monongahela Village. He never said a word about it to me. Then when we were talking about leaving to come here, he told me the canoe and all his trade goods are mine. He married Corn Stalk and says he has found his future. I was taken fully by surprise. Bright Moon says their hearts beat as one, as do mine and hers. I know you and him—"

Painted Turtle interrupted. "Were nothing more than good friends who enjoyed one another's bodies. His heart and mine did not beat as one. Wolf Chaser lost everything he had. As a friend, I took him in. Believe me, I had competition for him.

As the days went by, we gradually found a mutual need for each other. I still feel sorry for his loss, but his presence in my life makes me feel complete for the first time in many sun cycles."

"I am happy for all of you then. The moment I laid eyes on Bright Moon, I knew my heart was lost. I had heard rumors of her and her deeds up to that point, but I had no idea that she would have such a profound effect on me. God put her in my life and me in hers. I am convinced of that. In Cahokia, they claimed it was their "Sky Gods" who used us to make some prophecy of theirs come true. I only know that when I saw her, I knew I had a reason to live." He smiled contentedly.

"She is quite the warrior if all your stories are to be believed. Most of our young men would be either intimidated by her or try to dominate her. I do not think that would end well. I am glad you found a woman worthy of you. But do you think it is wise to take her off into the wilderness?"

"The thing about Bright Moon is that no one takes her anywhere. She goes where and when she wants. I am just thankful that she chooses my companionship. She can outshoot me with a bow or bola and outfight me with a war club and knife. But her dedication to me is stronger than the hardest granite. I am thankful to God she is in my life. Yes, if any two people can do something impossible, we will do it."

"Amazing!" Painted Turtle shook her head in disbelief. "But will you at least stay here for the winter so you won't be out in the forest somewhere with snow piled up over your heads and no food to be found?"

"We were hoping you would ask. This is her first child. I want her around someone experienced in these matters."

"By the looks of her, you did not get here any too soon. See the way she keeps pushing her belly down, just below her ribs? That child is becoming restless and wants to get out into the world."

Two days later, Bright Moon was escorted off to the Turtle Clan women's house and surrounded by anxious women. Round Shell even eagerly pitched in, bringing blankets, and hauling water to be heated. They had a lot to get done, with the Gamwing beginning in ten and five days, and now a child to be delivered...by a guest of the Sakimaxkwe no less—everything had to be perfect.

With coaching from Silver Leaf, the Turtle Clan's old midwife, Bright Moon made it through a long and painful labor to deliver a healthy boy child. Her strong lower back and pelvic muscles were slow to yield in opening her birth canal. Bright Moon's cheeks and forehead were blemished with broken capillaries, burst from the long hours of strong contractions, and pushing the child into the world. But she never complained nor cried out. She would not allow herself any sign of weakness. Silver Leaf was astounded by her strength and endurance. "I have never seen a first-time mother go through such a long delivery without complaining about the pain." She handed the child back to his mother after washing him.

"And would complaining have made it any easier or faster, Grandmother?" Bright Moon smiled at her little man. As soon as he was in her arms, he eagerly found a nipple and began to nurse. He also flexed his little hands and legs, demonstrating his health and strength. In the dim light of the women's lodge in the middle of the night, it was difficult to tell his skin or eye color, but she could see that his thick, fuzzy hair was the color of beach sand.

It had been decided that a boy would be named "Erik" after Yellow Hair's deceased father. While among the peoples who spoke the Lenape tongue, he would be known as "Acorn," a name from Bright Moon's past.

By the time the Gamwing started, Bright Moon had returned to the Turtle Clan Longhouse and was gaining strength. She was still sore from the long labor and delivery but was eager to help in any way she could. She found she could stir gruel and nurse at the same time, which made her feel useful. When Acorn was sleeping she also took turns at the big log pestle crushing corn into meal in the large wooden mortar next to the longhouse. *I used to hate this job, but now I can feel it strengthening my shoulders, arms, and back. I will need my strength in the sun cycles to come.*

How lucky I am that these people have accepted me. I feel a part of Yellow Hair's adopted family. I could be happy here, I think. Were it not for our promise to find Yellow Hair's true family, I could be content staying here in Sun Town, Bright Moon thought, as she lifted the heavy oak pestle up and let it drop onto the corn kernels in the log mortar.

CHAPTER 5
NEW MUD TOWN

With the river clear of flowing ice and the last of the snow melted in the higher hills, it was time to move on. Red Oak and his men departed for Monongahela Village the day before Long Cat would lead Yellow Hair north.

Yellow Hair had warned Wolf Chaser that Ganeco was not dead and would probably be out to seek revenge for last summer's little war walk against Yellow Hair that ended badly for him. Wolf Chaser dismissed Ganeco, saying, "That maneater will never gather enough warriors to cross the mountains into our territory. And if he does, we will be ready for him."

"All of the elders tell me you were the most popular storyteller at the Gamwing. Are you sure you do not want to stay and tell more? The Willet Villagers could not get enough of your tales." Painted Turtle continued to tease Yellow Hair in hopes he would elect to stay in Sun Town.

"I need to go have some more adventures before I have any more tales to tell. It was good to see them, though. I suppose old Wattle and Long Beard will be gone if we ever come back this way. I feel bad they were not here for Gamwing.

"And I am afraid that when Wattle fails, Willet Village will be overrun by Lenape Town, and we will lose another of the river people villages."

"Bear Claw is strong. He and Red Feather will be a match for Lenape Town,"

———

BRIGHT MOON LET Peeper nurse one last time before she handed him back to Willow Branch. Peeper was born in midwinter, so he was three moons younger than Acorn. Bright Moon always produced more milk than Acorn needed, so she nursed Peeper when Willow Branch was busy. The mothers had become quite attached to each other's children, and these last goodbyes were difficult.

Strong Wing decided he and Loose Arrow would take a canoe as far as New Mud Town so they could wait to say goodbye. In actuality, he did not want Willow Branch, Painted Turtle, and Wolf Chaser to see him with tears in his eyes when Yellow Hair left forever again.

Finally, the three canoes were loaded, and Acorn was passed around one more time among the women who had come to adore him with his light skin, sandy hair, and big blue eyes. He would have Bright Moon's sharp chin and narrow face with high cheekbones, but Yellow Hair clearly lived in him. That made Bright Moon love him all the more, if that was possible.

The three canoes shoved off from the Sun Town landing in the middle of the Awakening Moon. Late on the fourth day, they saw smoke rising above the palisade surrounding New Mud Town where it sat on a hill overlooking its corn fields. The palisade logs had faded to a light gray, but still looked new.

"Hoo!" a warrior called from the lead of four canoes of four warriors each that quickly closed on them.

As soon as the warrior recognized Strong Wing, he smiled and shouted, "Friends!"

The other warriors relaxed and began to unstring their bows.

From one of the other canoes, Green Snake

shouted, "Look, it is Yellow Hair! We thought you were gone forever!"

"I came back to teach you how to shoot that bow, Green Snake!"

Long into the night Yellow Hair was telling his stories of the time he was gone.

"You wounded Ganeco?" Otter asked in awe. "You are a good shot, why did you not just kill him?"

"I was not sure of his strength. I did know that if we wounded someone in each canoe, they would have to tend to them, and not come after us. I thought by just wounding him, he would still be in command and do the wise thing. I worry that he will send warriors this way in revenge though."

"We have handled him in the past, we will in the future. If you find your way, he will no longer be of your concern. Enough talk for one night. Let us rest."

The next day, while relaxing under Saki-maxkwe Sweet Water's sunshade, she said to Yellow Hair, "My heart is glad that Traveler has finally found happiness in the arms of a woman. I have always feared he would die a horrible death at the hands of some chief who did not honor trade or in an accident on some lonely stretch of river. Now at least, he will be in the hands of a clan, cared for."

"I always thought he preferred the former, so it was a total surprise to me when he said he was staying in Monongahela Village,"

"Men! I knew he was going back to Corn Stalk before we even got to Cahokia."

"How?" Yellow Hair asked in disbelief.

"I saw the way he looked at us. He knew he had that with her, and I could tell he would seek the first chance to get back to her." She shrugged her shoulders like it was common knowledge.

Acorn started to fuss in the arms of Sweet Water's ten-summers-old daughter, Down. She was holding him awkwardly on her skinny hip while trying to play a hoop and stick game with her friends. As Down handed Acorn back to Bright Moon, she pouted. "I will never be a good mother."

"You have much time to learn."

"She dotes on every child in the village." Sweet Water shook her head while she watched her daughter play the game. "She will be a great mother."

"Just like her mother," Bright Moon offered. "They learn from what they see."

"How did you learn? You saw death and destruction as a child," Sweet Water asked as Yellow Hair, Long Cat, and Otter walked down to the river to join some of the other men.

"I saw those things, but I also remember my

mother's kindness and love. I have seen what kind of mothers bring loving children into adulthood and which ones do not. I want my child to be the loving kind. Wolf guides my actions when I need him most, but I know he also wants me to be a loving wife and mother."

"You are a remarkable young woman. Yellow Hair is lucky to have found you."

"Oh, I think there was no *finding*, as you say. I think Power put us together like the head and handle of a war club. We were shaped and honed for each other before we met and then were fitted together and bound by the strong sinews and thongs of love before we had a chance to even ponder it." Bright Moon smiled as she wondered where the words came from that flowed from her mouth.

————

"So, tell me Yellow Hair, how is it that you are going to find this great canoe you are seeking? My understanding is that far in the north, there are few trees and very few people. You could end up starving in such a place. And the winters, I have heard, are more savage than anyone here can imagine. How can anyone eke out a living in such desolate conditions?" Otter looked over Yellow

Hair's canoe for any wear and tear that needed attention.

"Long Cat has trade connections that will lead us to the place where my grandfather's canoe comes to trade. There is no mistake that the cloth hat Long Cat keeps in his personal bag was woven on a loom on my grandfather's farm in Greenland. He is a very powerful chief. He will see to it that I have an important place in his clan. My family will be well cared for once we arrive. This long journey will be worth the effort. If I am given the chance, you will see a Norse great canoe bringing fine trade goods to this landing. Those people have no idea what a wealth of skins and fine jewels are waiting to be found and bargained for in these lands. I intend to open a great trade exchange between our peoples that will be beneficial to all of us." Yellow Hair hoped he was not premature in expressing his dream.

"But what of the stories of your people being warriors who kill our relatives with no remorse for even trying to bargain?"

"I know some Norsemen have been unworthy of being called that. There is always that kind among all peoples. Let us not forget Thunder Throat or Ganeco. The pure-hearted men and women must prevail to make life better for all. We can accomplish so much more through peaceful transactions than by conquering each other."

"Your words speak the truth and carry wisdom, Yellow Hair. I pray that you can prevail in your ambitions. I will remember that you said these words here today. But I will not share them for I do not wish to prepare my people for something that never happens. Legend has it that your people have caused more harm than good in their dealings with the northern peoples. I will wait to see the good for myself before I make my judgment. You are a good man and have a good heart. Find others like yourself, then bring them here, and we will trade."

"That I will. You are a fair and just man. So are many of the others I have met in my travels. But the blood on my hands tells me that there are people everywhere with dark hearts. If I cannot bring light to these lands, I will not come. I promise you that."

"Then I look forward to our next meeting." Otter put a hand on Yellow Hair's shoulder.

That night in the Heron Clan longhouse owned by Sweet Water, a great feast was laid out in honor of the travelers. Yellow Hair, Bright Moon, and Long Cat shared more stories of their adventures traveling to Cahokia and back. The descriptions of the great mounds being built and planned in

Cahokia were spellbinding to people who had never seen them. The sheer number of people needed to accomplish such feats was hard to imagine. Yet, every trader who came through had been talking about the throngs of people moving or planning to move to the Cahokia area. What they had not believed before, they did after these trusted sources spoke of the wonders along the Grandfather River.

"Tomorrow, when you four are headed upriver, our women, girls, and young boys will be in the fields with our hoes and root sticks preparing to plant corn. With the Solstice Celebration in Willet Village this year, we need to have our crops in early." With that, everyone started preparing for sleep.

The next morning, more long goodbyes were exchanged at the canoe landing. This time Strong Wing did not care who saw tears in his eyes. He and Loose Arrow shoved off downstream first while the others continued hugging and promising good health and happiness upon those they were seeing for the last time.

CHAPTER 6

ROUND TRACK VILLAGE

Yellow Hair had once confided in Bright Moon that he had gotten to know a maiden from Round Track Village. He hoped that his description of Stinger as fiercely competitive and very athletic was not going to set up some sort of a jealous confrontation between Bright Moon and Stinger. Stinger's husband, whom he expected had beat her in the past, could be a problem as well. The way he played pahsahë-men, he might be the jealous type as well. If Stinger told him about coupling with Yellow Hair, then he might want a turn at Bright Moon in return. That would not happen. So, with some angst, he pushed the canoe into the canoe landing next to the two canoes full of warriors who had escorted them the past hand of time. The banter between Long Cat and the warriors was friendly so Yellow Hair was able to relax a bit.

Round Track Village was not surrounded by a palisade, and the lodges seemed to blend right into the fields where dozens of topless women, girls, and young boys were planting corn, the first of the three sisters to be put in the ground.

"Long Cat! It is rumored that the Haudenosaunee ate you, or was it the Illini? Either way, it is a surprise to see you at Round Track!" A burly warrior stomped up and hugged the trader, laughing as he spoke.

"Big Track, my heart sings to see you! Meet my friends. The yellow-haired one is Yellow Hair, he has so many clans, I will let him tell you his lineage. The woman is Yellow Hair's wife, Bright Moon. She has a long history as well. But the pup is Acorn, and he belongs to Bright Moon." Long Cat was not used to saying so many words at one time unless it was about some trade item.

"We have seen this Yellow Hair before. He plays pahsahëmen pretty well. He also kills Minquas for sport and travels far. And the woman, Bright Moon, has a reputation as a serious mankiller, but with the pup in her arms, she looks pretty harmless. Ha-ha!" Big Track guffawed. "Sakimaxkwe Squash is down at the planting fields right now. If she was expecting such famous guests, she would have a feast prepared. We expect some hunters back this day with fresh venison. If your palates are not too spoiled on clams and oysters, it should be tolerable."

"We are passing through upriver and just wanted to drop by and give our respects. We wish to cause no burden on your village, Big Track."

"Nonsense, Long Cat! You will rest here a couple of days if I have to feed you myself. The women are trying to get the planting done early so they have plenty of time to make fancy things to take to Willet Village for the Solstice. But some can spare a day or two to entertain the likes of you." Big Track waved to include the four of them.

"The hospitality of Round Track is appreciated." Yellow Hair nodded to Big Track. A movement caught his eye, and he turned to see a boy running up from the field many of the women were planting.

Out of breath, the boy wheezed, "Squash wishes to know who comes to Round Track." The boy barely got it out before he put his hands on his knees and heaved trying to get his breath.

Tell her, "Friends!" Big Track chuckled. The boy started back toward the field at a slow trot.

Six hunters brought in three deer, and a feast was hastily put together in honor of the guests.

The feast was held in the plaza where everyone in the village could attend and hear the stories. Yellow Hair presented Squash with a bundle of fox skins for her hospitality. Once again, stories told by Yellow Hair, Bright Moon, and Long Cat went far into the night. Suddenly the tales of exotic travel and far-off places outweighed the need to plant the three sisters. Those corn seeds could sit another day or two before they were stuck in the ground.

At one point while Bright Moon was telling her mountain lion story. Yellow Hair felt a sense of pride at how well she could communicate in her broken Lenape. He even had difficulties with some of the words used here in Round Track, as their dialect was different than that used in Sun Town, and even more so than Willet Village. Long Cat had to act as an interpreter for both Yellow Hair and Bright Moon at times while they told their tales. But Bright Moon learned remarkably fast.

He felt a person nudge in beside him. "She is beautiful," Stinger stated matter-of-factly, looking at Bright Moon. She was leaner than Yellow Hair remembered from the last time he saw her. He noted she was missing a couple teeth, and her jaw was swollen. Her left cheek displayed a large bruise, and her right eye looked like it was almost healed from being blackened. A scar over her right eye and another on her left cheek indicated past injuries. The scar from her bee sting had faded on her right cheek, but it was still visible, as was the scar from their heads banging in the pahsahëmen game several sun cycles past.

"You look like you have been playing pahsahëmen with your head again." He tried to keep it light but could not hold his anger that her husband would beat her like that.

She smiled, showing the gaps in her teeth. "The price of being married to a great warrior. It is nothing."

"No!" He raised his voice. "It is not 'nothing!' It sounds like your husband needs to be taught how a woman is to be treated."

"I fail to please him sometimes. It is nothing, and it is none of your business…" Suddenly she was yanked away. She stumbled and fell, but Long Scar kept walking, dragging her like a rag doll. Long Scar's name came from the scar running from his hip to his knee. He had been returning from his vision quest as part of his initiation into manhood when he slipped on a muddy riverbank getting back to his canoe. As he slid down the bank, a sharp rock sliced his skin, exposing the muscles and tendons along his leg. He was able to drag himself into his canoe and float the three hands of time back to Round Track

Village where he was tended by a great healer. The injury, as gruesome as it looked, did not cause any permanent damage beyond an ugly scar.

Yellow Hair followed and grabbed Long Scar by the shoulder and turned him around to face him. "Someone needs to teach you how to treat a woman." Yellow Hair squared and crouched, prepared for a fight.

Long Scar grabbed Stinger by the arm and lifted her to her feet and said, "Let us go!"

Again, Yellow Hair spun Long Scar around and glared at him.

"I will not kill a guest of the Sakimaxkwe. Go back to your storytelling, turd."

Just then Big Track stepped between them. "What is this all about?" The big man looked from Yellow Hair to Long Scar to Stinger.

"Wandering Fool, here thought he would plant his manhood in my wife. I am trying to get her away from him," Long Scar said, loud enough for many to hear.

"That is a lie. I asked her how she got those bruises on her face. He came along and dragged her off."

"Ask her." Long Scar nodded at Stinger, who stood massaging her arm and looking at the ground. "Well?" he yelled at her.

"It...it...it...is as my husband says," she barely whispered.

Seeing the situation, Squash stepped in. "Stinger, did this man hurt you?" She pointed to Yellow Hair.

"N...no."

"What is going on here, Long Scar? I saw you drag Stinger away from the storytelling. Why?"

"As I told Big Track, this foreign worm tried to get her to go off into the shadows while his woman was telling her story."

"You know this how? I was looking at Stinger talking to Yellow Hair. There is no way you could have heard what they were saying. You just walked up and grabbed her by the arm and started dragging her off. What is going on here?"

"I will not listen to this talk from you or anyone else. This man is a foreign snake and deserves to die. All right, I will fight him—to the death—with knives! I will be glad to rid the world of his filth!" Stinger looked as if she would slink away if Long Scar did not have a tight grip on her arm.

"You are talking like your souls are loose, Long Scar. You need to calm down." Squash tried to reason with him.

Bright Moon stood beside Yellow Hair, but she had her eyes on Long Scar's. She had seen that look before. A predator, ready to strike. She watched his eyes flashing from person to person, assessing his options.

"I will not fight you with knives…"

"Coward! I told you he was a cowardly turd!"

"I will fight you with no weapons. If Long Scar yields to Yellow Hair, Stinger will divorce him immediately, he will be outcast from Round Track Village, and Yellow Hair will take Long Scar north into the wilderness as a slave."

"And if Yellow Hair yields to Long Scar, Yellow Hair will leave Round Track immediately, he can take that little bag of worm puss with him, and the woman becomes Long Scar's second wife."

Yellow Hair tried to think of a way out of that last part. "Long Scar does not deserve one wife, much less two! Yellow Hair…"

"…accepts these terms." Bright Moon spoke up, giving Long Scar an enigmatic smile.

"What are you doing?" Yellow Hair whispered to her while keeping his eye on Long Scar, who looked at Bright Moon with lust in his eyes.

"Just giving you more incentive to break that fool. Do not worry, if by some chance you lose the fight, Long Scar will not live to see the sunrise," she whispered back while smiling coyly toward Long Scar.

"I will not fail you," Yellow Hair whispered, not

quite as confidently as he wanted to sound. Long Scar looked like he knew how to fight.

"I know." Then added, "Watch his eyes closely, they will betray his movements before he makes them."

"Combatants to the center of the plaza. Watchers form a ring large enough for them to fight!" Big Track took control of the awkward situation. When everyone had assembled, he walked up to Yellow Hair and said, "Take off your shirt and moccasins. Then take off your breechclout and hand it to me for inspection." Satisfied that Yellow Hair hid no weapons, he handed him back his breechclout and told him to put it back on, then turned to Long Scar and gave the same order.

"You have known me my whole life, War Chief, there is no need to search me like that foreign intruder." Long Scar smiled at Big Track like they were old friends.

"I will search you nonetheless, warrior," Big Track answered coolly.

Long Scar complied. Big Track pulled a small, sharp, bone stiletto and a small chert blade from pockets in Long Scar's breechclout.

Long Scar shrugged his shoulders and said, "I have been looking for those. I thought I had lost them."

"Sakimaxkwe Squash, I have inspected the

combatants for weapons. Note that the stranger, Yellow Hair, had none, while the warrior, Long Scar, had a stiletto and a chert blade hidden in his breechclout. Both men are now free of weapons, and the fight can begin. The terms are the two men will fight, unaided, until one or the other yields. If Yellow Hair yields to Long Scar, he and his boy child will make ready and set off upriver as soon as possible. The woman, Bright Moon, will move into maid Stinger's lodge as Long Scar's second wife. If Long Scar yields to Yellow Hair..."

Long Scar interrupted, "That will not happen!"

Big Track continued as if Long Scar had not interrupted, "Maid Stinger will immediately move Long Scar's possessions from her lodge and divorce him. Long Scar will accompany Yellow Hair upriver as a slave. At your command, Saki-maxkwe, the fight will begin," Big Track addressed the crowd and Squash.

"The combatants will stand before me." When they complied, Squash went on, "Never have I seen two complete strangers with so much animosity toward each other. There is more to this story than we have heard here tonight." She looked directly into Stinger's eyes. "I expect you know more than you are willing to say. And I expect you to say it to me before this night is over. Let the best man win. The fight shall begin!"

Yellow Hair and Long Scar slowly circled, facing one another, sizing up their opponent. Cheers and jeers came from a small group of Long Scar's friends scattered around the circle. No one spoke up on Yellow Hair's behalf. Yellow Hair focused on Long Scar's eyes. Bright Moon was correct, he could see the man assessing his options. Long Scar's focus locked on Yellow Hair's right leg. Yellow Hair made sure each step was the same as the last, lulling Long Scar into thinking how he would move.

Long Scar lunged, trying to grab Yellow Hair's right leg. But Yellow Hair knew the move was coming, quickly moved his leg back and drove a fist into the back of Long Scar's upper arm. Long Scar reeled and stepped back, rubbing the deep bruise on his arm. Anger filled his eyes. He charged directly at Yellow Hair. The two big men locked arms, pushing and shoving, looking for advantage. After several heartbeats with no one getting an upper hand, they backed off and stared at each other. Sweat now flowed down both of their chests. Long Scar's wolf tattoo on his chest seemed to be breathing along with him as his chest heaved.

Yellow Hair feigned to his right and swept in, grabbing Long Scar's right shin, and lifting it off the ground. Long Scar reacted and broke his foot loose from Yellow Hair's grasp, kicking him in the side. Yellow Hair flinched at the pain and stepped back. Long Scar, thinking he had an advantage, charged in trying to take Yellow Hair to the ground. Yellow Hair recalled a move he learned as a boy, of throwing a shield upward into an opponent's chest. He slammed his forearm into Long Scar's sternum with all his strength. The blow took Long Scar's breath away, and he fell to the ground gasping. Yellow Hair rolled him to his back and lifted his waist off the ground with his breechclout thongs. That position brought Long Scar's breath back in deep gasps. Yellow Hair dropped Long Scar's waist back to the ground and settled in behind him and wrapped his powerful arm around Long Scar's neck from behind.

"Yield?" Yellow Hair gasped.

"No!" Long Scar replied, kicking and flailing his arms to no avail.

Yellow Hair squeezed harder. "Yield?!"

"No!" Long Scar rasped.

Yellow Hair squeezed harder. "Yield?!"

"No," Long Scar barely squeaked. "Kill me."

"Kill was not in the terms! Yield!" Yellow Hair ordered. His arms were becoming strained holding his powerful adversary.

"No," Long Scar squeaked again.

Yellow Hair squeezed harder. Finally, Long Scar

fell limp. Yellow Hair loosed his hold and again lifted Long Scar's waist off the ground until he choked a breath. Yellow Hair dropped him again and turned to Squash. Heaving, he said, between breaths, "Sakimaxkwe Squash, the terms of this combat were not to kill. I cannot kill this man. If he will not yield, I ask you to decide his fate, but I do not wish to kill him myself. He is a complete stranger to me, and I hold no animosity for him other than he is a wife-beater, which I find egregious."

Squash was in deep contemplation and looked at Big Track when Stinger rose and stepped forward. She pulled a hand-long bone stiletto from her apron and said to Squash, "I will do it."

Squash looked at Stinger for several heartbeats. "If anyone has cause to kill this man, it is you. I ask only that you make it quick. He has suffered enough." Long Scar was the son of a cousin to Squash. But then, Stinger was distantly related as well, along with many of the residents of Round Track Village.

Long Scar had partially recovered and was sitting up, holding his painful neck. "You cannot kill your husband, the father of your son." He smirked as his broken voice squeaked out the words.

"Lest you get any ideas." Big Track squatted

behind Long Scar, pulled his arms behind his back, and bound them with a strip of rawhide.

Stinger walked over and kneeled next to Long Scar. "How does it feel to be the helpless one?"

"You can still yield," Yellow Hair said from where he stood next to Bright Moon, who was checking out his bruised ribs.

"Never!" Long Scar's voice cracked.

Without hesitation, Stinger plunged her stiletto into Long Scar's heart. He tensed, eyes fully open, looking at her in disbelief. Dark red blood pumped from the wound and pink foam sprayed from the hole with each shallow breath. Quickly his life drained from his body, and he slumped to the side without another word. A last breath cracked through his broken throat as he expired. A single tear rolled down Stinger's face.

Yellow Hair helped her to her feet and said, "He will never hurt you again."

"No, he will not," she whispered. As she looked at the corpse of her husband, she said, "It was not all bad, you know. We had good times. He...he just...he...hated it that he was not the only one who ever had me. He especially hated you because I spoke kindly of you, and he had no way to make you pay for giving me pleasure. That ate at him every day, for all these sun cycles. His souls were sick, and he was getting worse." Tears dripped off her face as she looked down.

"Now you can find someone who will treat you as you deserve to be treated," Yellow Hair consoled her.

"I deserve to be treated like a mankiller!" she cried.

"No, you just brought order to your life. Go to the Solstice Celebration in Willet Village, start your life over. You deserve happiness," he said softly.

"I have fields to take care of." She turned and walked into the night.

"Big Track, have someone take the body to the Wolf Clan charnel house. Yellow Hair and Bright Moon, a word with you. Everyone else, it is late. Go to your lodges, get some sleep. Tomorrow we have planting to do." Squash dispersed the crowded plaza. Most people were standing around in small groups discussing what had just taken place.

From somewhere in the darkness, a voice called out, "Yellow Hair, beware! There is a price on your head now."

Squash turned to Yellow Hair. "What are your plans? How soon can you leave? Under the circumstances, I would say sooner rather than later would be better."

"Sakimaxkwe, we are humbled and grateful for your hospitality. We will leave at first light if that is not too late for your liking. I am very sorry for how things turned out here tonight."

"The dead warrior earned his fate. What happened between you and Stinger that made him so jealous?"

"At the Solstice in Sun Town, six sun cycles past, she and I met head-to-head in the pahsahëmen game, you may remember. Later that night we came to know each other. She refused to let me fall in love with her. I had not talked to her since then. She was married when the Solstice Celebration was held in Round Track Village, and I only saw her from a distance. Apparently, she said kind words about me to her husband, and he became enraged and wanted me dead ever since. That is all I know."

"I will talk to her more. There are men who will want to take her as a second wife. She will be all right. You should look to your wife and child. Let me know if you need help loading your canoes in the morning. I am ready for sleep."

"Your counseling with Stinger did not go so well?" Bright Moon asked coyly.

"You know how she feels after killing a man."

"I hope I never have to kill my own husband. But I would if he treated me like hers did."

"You know you do not have to worry about that."

She took his hand and stared into his eyes. "I know."

"My moon did not arrive. Another child grows in my womb." She smiled into his eyes.

"It will be born in midwinter. I hope we are in comfortable surroundings when that happens."

"It will be all right."

CHAPTER 7
OVER THE PASS

Soon enough they were out of sight of Round Track Village and once again heading to an uncertain future. As they paddled upriver, they noted little changes in the terrain and forest. It was the river growing narrower and the current stronger that told them they were moving higher on the land, but little else changed.

Acorn was becoming more restless as the days became longer and hotter. He was no longer content to spend most of his day strapped to Bright Moon's chest so that he could suckle as he wished. Now he wanted to be out from under her oversized hunter's shirt where both he and she were constantly drenched in sweat. Bright Moon finally took her shirt off so he could breathe the fresh air. Air that was already too humid and was getting warmer each day. The afternoon heat and humidity were becoming oppressive, while paddling against the fast-moving river was increasingly difficult and strenuous. The cradle-board Yellow Hair fashioned from a flat piece of birch with buckskin straps gave Acorn a place where he could see his surroundings and kept him safely secured. That and a polished piece of deer femur to chew on kept him occupied much of the time.

Long Cat discussed the plan for getting them to the far north while they moved along. "The Mahican lands will carry you to the upper reaches of the Great River. But the lands north of there are controlled by Haudenosaunee speaking people who constantly make war on the Mahicans. After your little 'game' with Ganeco, I can imagine there is a heavy price on your head among the Haudenosaunee peoples. You will need to follow the Mahican trails east and north from there. I have no knowledge of those trails. I presume you will be able to trade your canoe for a guide to lead you to the great canoe landing that your people use. The trip will be a long one that will take you through lands controlled by the Abenaki, Maliseet, and Micmac from what I have been told. But they are all Algonkian speakers, so you should get along all right. Save some of those Cahokia-painted shells, and they will probably do anything you ask.

"I know a trader named Broken Bow who claims to know a trader who dealt with your people. He is the one I got that woven hat from that you say came from your grandfather's clan. If I can get you connected to him, he will get you where you want to go. I will leave you in Cold Water Creek Village. It lies a day's float down Cold Water Creek on the far side of that pass just up ahead. It will take us two days to portage all our things to that creek. It is fast and rocky in the upper stretches, but no worse than what I have seen you two handle in the past."

"This Broken Bow, how will we find him? If he is a trader, he could be anywhere."

"I am sure that by now he has heard that I am bringing you into the Mahican lands, and he will probably be waiting for us in Cold Water Creek Village."

"How could word get upriver? I have seen no one pass us."

"There are ways men talk without being in physical contact with one another. News always travels faster than a man can paddle a canoe—you should know that."

"But we have seen no one since we left Round

Track three days past. How could a message travel without a man to carry it?"

"Men and boys who know the trails can move faster than canoes can follow a river, especially upriver. I am sure Traveler taught you that."

"Yes, of course, but I did not realize that Round Track cared if we went upriver or down. I did not think Squash would alert Cold Water Creek Village that we were coming. Why would they care?"

"Why would they care? You are joking? Yellow Hair's arrival, disappearance, and return are the biggest news this river valley has heard in a lifetime. Throw in Bright Moon, the mankiller, and you have a sensation. Everyone wants to be part of the story." Long Cat felt like he was relaying old news.

"Do people still call me 'Cass'?" Bright Moon had disbelief in her voice.

"Cass destroyed an invincible war chief. Bright Moon is the name they do not know."

"I thought that story would be buried by now."

"Your story will outlive you by many sun cycles, woman. You are a legend. The tale will only grow grander. One day they will tell the story of *Cass, the forbidden woman warrior, who killed ten tens of armed warriors with her bare hands just to get to an evil Manitou.* Of course, there are others who will want to say that they brought an inglorious end to the evil witch, Cass. No, your story is not buried yet."

Bright Moon just shook her head and looked at Acorn who was now at her breast.

———

BEFORE DARK, they were camped at the canoe landing next to the trail that led over the pass to Cold Water Creek. The day had started unbearably hot with no wind, but as they climbed upstream, the cooler water moderated the air temperature somewhat. After the sun finished its journey into the west, lightning began to light the western sky. By the middle of the night, the storm had dissipated to a steady, soaking rain. The violence of the thunderstorm they expected to last into the night had fizzled.

The next morning was met with heavy warm air and a muddy trail that meandered steeply up and over the pass. They spent the whole day carrying the canoes over the pass and to the landing on Cold Water Creek, which was suitably named for cold water springs at its headwaters. They sorely missed Red Oak's warriors' help with the most difficult portage they had encountered since leaving Cahokia. The air was humid and hazy, giving them a poor look at the green valley that lay before them. On a clear day, they would be able to see the smoke rising from fires in Cold Water Creek Village. Yellow Hair and Bright Moon would have to take Long Cat's word that it was down there. That night they spent in the same camp as the night before. The following night was at a landing along Cold Water Creek where many had camped over the sun cycles.

Moving down Cold Water Creek was treacherous at first with the fast-moving water and numerous large rocks in the channel. They had to portage around a few of the more dangerous rapids and waterfalls. By the second afternoon they had an escort of two canoes with five young men each. The canoes were made of bark and built similar to Yellow Hair's. The warriors knew Long Cat and were friendly once they recognized him.

They made camp at a suitable place just before dark. One of the canoes of warriors joined them while the other continued on to the village. The warriors shared a fresh-killed deer they had taken earlier in the afternoon. Stories were told around the campfire, and the young warriors stared in awe at Yellow Hair and Bright Moon. They had heard the names and versions of their stories, but to sit at the same campfire with such legends was unthinkable.

Acorn practiced using his newly arrived teeth

to bite off soft pieces of roasted venison and suck on them until he could swallow the meat. He preferred the corn cakes he would get every time they stopped at a village or farmstead. He was proud of his biting abilities, though he had found out a couple of moons earlier that biting Mama's nipple was not a welcome practice. She pinched his nose each time he decided to bite, pinching harder each successive time. It did not take him long to learn not to do that. He was also trying out his voice now, and even trying to say words, which came out as gibberish. It would not be long before he would be ready to walk.

CHAPTER 8

COLD CREEK VILLAGE

By early the next afternoon the three canoes pulled onto the landing below Cold Water Creek Village. Like New Mud Town, this village was located on a hill overlooking crop fields that had been planted less than ten days before. Most of the plants were just breaking the surface giving the fields a greenish cast. The village itself was surrounded by a palisade.

Once inside, Yellow Hair noted that the village was very similar in appearance to the Lenape villages he was used to. There were ten-and-three longhouses arranged in three clusters surrounding a central plaza with a single large pole and a large fire pit. The clusters of longhouses represented the Wolf, Deer, and Bear Clans. The largest, he was told, belonged to Tall Woman, the *Sachem* of the village. It bore the wolf symbol and the red and black face of the Creator god. Yellow Hair assumed the big longhouse also served as the Big House for the Gamwing. Tall Woman only talked once the formal introductions were completed.

"Welcome to our humble village, great travelers. We hope our hospitality meets your expectations." Yellow Hair was pleasantly surprised that he understood nearly every word in her phrases. She sounded as if she had been raised in Round Track Village. "We will feast before listening to your stories in the plaza, well into the night. Brave Wolf, see to it that there are enough smoke fires to drive away the mosquitoes." A young man of about ten-and-six summers left the longhouse.

Soon they were seated around the central fire pit in the Wolf Clan longhouse. The fire pit was cold due to the warm daytime temperatures. Light was provided by pitch torches along the sides of the fire pit. Pots of venison stew, bark plates of corn and acorn cakes, and ceramic cups of sassafras and mint tea were presented to each person by servants. Following the meal, the servants collected the wooden bowls and ceramic cups.

The conversation around the feast was kept light, focusing on the weather, the prospects for another good harvest in the fall and plentiful game in the surrounding forests. No mention was made of war, death, or sickness. After the food was consumed and everyone satisfied with the sleeping arrangements, Tall Woman announced that they would move out into the plaza to hear the travelers' tales.

Outside, a veil of cedar smoke filled the air and stung the eyes. But at least the clouds of mosquitoes were kept at bay. Long Cat stood by to act as interpreter as needed. Yellow Hair was able to convey his stories with little help, but Bright Moon had more difficulty getting everyone to understand her Monongahela accent. She could say most of the Munsee words, but her voice inflections were somewhat foreign to them. The villagers were in awe of the stories they heard from the visitors. They had all heard the legends of Yellow Hair and his woman's adventures, but to hear them from the actual people who lived those things was most amazing. Many shook their heads in disbelief. Acorn provided a side show as he crawled from one young maiden to the next, giggling and touching their babies, making them laugh.

Finally, Tall Woman signaled that the night was over, and everyone filed off to their own lodges. Once inside the Wolf Clan longhouse, they found their bedding laid out on sleeping platforms along the south wall.

"Sachem, we would gladly sleep on the floor. We do not wish to displace anyone from their bed platform."

"It is no trouble. I hope you do not think so lowly of Cold Water Creek Village that we let our honored guests sleep on the floor! Make yourselves comfortable. Bright Moon, a word with you please." She led Bright Moon through a woven reed door hanging that led to the Sachem's private sleeping quarters at the west end of the longhouse.

"Do you feel for your child's safety while traveling so far into the unknown?" Tall Woman asked Bright Moon slowly to make sure she understood each word.

"Acorn is growing stronger each day. He will be walking, I think, before the fall equinox." Bright Moon tried to say as clearly as she could.

"No, I mean the child growing in your womb." Tall Woman pointed to Bright Moon's belly.

"I am with child. How did you know? I have just barely missed one moon, have not even felt sick in the morning."

"I need only look upon your face, child. A woman just knows these things. I fear you will not find any great canoes before winter sets in. They say in the far north, winter comes much earlier, and with much more ferocity than we experience here. How will you manage if you are between villages and a great storm sweeps down upon you?" Tall Woman spoke with serious concern in her voice.

"My husband has experience with the north and the winters, I leave those problems to him. He speaks of great lodges with roaring fires and endless feasting." Bright Moon spoke with more confidence than she felt.

"You have to get there first. I will worry about your well-being always. I have known you for about ten hands of time and feel like you are one of my daughters. Do you always ingratiate yourself to others like this?"

"Not hardly. It seems I have made many enemies. I only wanted to kill one man. Unfortunately, I have found myself defending someone I love, or myself, all too often. But do not worry about me. Wolf, my spirit helper assures me I will raise many children in Yellow Hair's lands across the great water. He tells me that once we leave Turtle Island, he can no longer protect me. I will always need to be vigilant and strong," Bright Moon answered evenly, with no fear in her voice.

"May the Great Manitou rest on your shoulder and guide you throughout your journey." Tall Woman put a hand on Bright Moon's shoulder.

"I have Wolf—First Man. I can ask for no better protector. Every time I have been in a bad situation, he appears, and time slows down for me. I can see the action I need to take, and it comes easily to me. I am blessed to have him on my side."

"Amazing."

From the outer room, the sound of Acorn crying got the women's attention. "Feeding time!"

The next morning, while taking their morning gruel and tea, Long Cat looked to One Wolf, Tall Woman's husband and War Chief of Cold Water Creek Village. "Have you seen the trader Broken Bow this season? I was hoping we would find him here."

One Wolf looked sideways at Long Cat and said, "He trades out of the Haudenosaunee lands north of the Great River headwaters. He is born of their blood. Do you trust him?"

"I have known him several sun cycles, he seems an honest sort. He is widely traveled, and my friends here need his help finding their way into the northern lands."

"Solstice will arrive in half a moon, he always seems to show up several days in advance with some exotic skins, ivory, copper, and other things we cannot find in these lands. If he follows his pattern, he will be here soon." One Wolf showed a bit of contempt in his voice.

"I assume he comes down the Great River. I wonder if we might intercept him in another village before he gets here. I have never been upriver from here and do not know any of the Sachems from the other *Muhhekuneuw* villages. Yellow Hair and Bright Moon need to get as far north as they can before winter sets in."

"Broken Bow enjoys his time at Solstice too much to forgo that to escort a couple of foreigners to some unknown place among the northern wild men." One Wolf scowled as he spoke.

"Great War Chief, we do not wish to overstay our welcome here among your people," Yellow Hair injected himself into the conversation.

"It is up to the Sachem to decide how long you are welcome, Yellow Hair. But I do not think she will tire of your stories anytime soon."

"Perhaps we can help on a hunt or with some other work around the village?" Yellow Hair offered.

"Yes, your bow sounds very accurate. Thankfully, we have no war in these lands at this time, but it sounds like all four of you would come in handy in a fight." One Wolf smiled.

"Bright Moon has the most accurate bow among us,"

"There will be stickball games at the Solstice. Can either of you play?" One Wolf asked coyly.

"I have watched some games. I have played

pahsahëman and chunkey. Do you have chunkey matches here?" Yellow Hair asked.

"Chunkey? Never heard of it. We let the southern people play pahsahëman. Stickball is our game. Not many sun cycles past, we averted a bloody conflict with some River Haudenosaunee with a stickball game. We beat them and a peace accord was reached. Of course, that has been forgotten by those maneaters since." One Wolf looked away before he finished. "What is chunkey?" He turned back to Yellow Hair.

"A game played on a smooth clay court. A player rolls a disk made of baked clay or carved rock, then he and/or his teammates throw a special spear to the place where they think it will roll to a stop. The one closest gets a point. Games are played to two-tens of points. Watchers bet on the players or teams. Sometimes the stakes get very high, up to and including wives or even someone's life. We witnessed some big matches in Cahokia."

"Witnessed?" Long Cat spoke up. "Yellow Hair here helped propel the Sun Clan team to the Great Harvest High Championship. Biggest match possible in that city or the world."

One Wolf smiled and nodded to Yellow Hair in admiration. "Tomorrow we will get out early before it gets hot and introduce you to stickball."

Over the next few days, Yellow Hair played stickball with the men while Bright Moon practiced with Tall Woman's daughters and the rest of the Wolf Clan's young maids and maidens. They both learned quickly and would participate in the Solstice games.

On a steamy day, a commotion rose down by the canoe landing. The shouts and calls signaled the arrival of the popular trader Broken Bow. Several of the young wives especially looked forward to his arrival. More than one husband would be asked to leave his lodge for a night while Broken Bow was in the village.

Seated at the fire pit in the plaza, Long Cat introduced Yellow Hair and Bright Moon to Broken Bow. "Ah, the famous Yellow Hair who destroyed Ganeco's war party down on the Juniata River. You do get around. Ganeco's last request was a mouthful of your heart. No one could find you, and he died hungry, so the story goes."

"Dead? Ganeco is dead? We left him wounded, not serious at that. How did he die?"

"The wound in his leg was invaded by demons, and his shaman could not drive them out. The other wounded men survived, have put a price on your head, and vowed to go on a war walk into the lower Mud River lands as soon as they gather strength. It would surprise them to find you here.

Lucky for you, the Long Lake People have no love for the dead war chief or his followers, and their war on you means nothing. In fact, among the more northern Haudenosaunee peoples, you are seen as a hero and welcome to their campfires."

"That is welcome news indeed. Do you have knowledge of where we might find the great winged canoes of my people, the Norsemen?" Yellow Hair pressed Broken Bow a bit anxiously.

"My friend, we have days to talk business before we go upriver. Relax and enjoy the good company of Tall Woman and her people. I will get you to your people, if they have done nothing stupid to get themselves all killed by their Micmac hosts. Now, tell me about this beautiful woman who sits at your side." It was clear Broken Bow thought very highly of himself and his ability to seduce women.

"Bright Moon is my wife of three sun cycles. She is the mother of my son, Acorn, and carries a second child in her womb." To anyone listening, Yellow Hair's voice betrayed his jealousy. Broken Bow was not listening.

"Yes, I know who she is, my friend. Her reputation travels as far and glorious as yours. She somehow does not have the look of a killer of men." Broken Bow looked at Bright Moon's eyes and smiled coyly.

"Bright Moon harms people only in defense of herself or those she loves, such as my husband." Bright Moon's eyes glared into the trader's eyes.

"Like the mother bear. You have great tales to tell, both of you. I look forward to hearing all of them in the coming days. I will see you through the Haudenosaunee lands to the Micmac who host your great canoe in the summer moons while they trade the animal-hair cloth for trees. But I must warn you, your brethren are becoming increasingly bothersome. The Micmac could cut off trade with them at any time. The fair-skinned people in the great canoes think they have more strength and cunning than the people they trade with. It is their mistake and will lead to their undoing."

"I understand and have been witness to that attitude. I believe my time with all the peoples I have encountered since I was washed ashore in the Lenape lands will guide me in teaching my people how to respect and trade fairly with all the people they meet."

"Someone with your experience and wisdom may help make things better. I wish you success. Now I need to catch up with some old friends. We will talk more." Broken Bow got up and wandered among the Cold Water Creek Village crowd that had gathered around the plaza. Yellow Hair was impressed how the young trader spoke many tongues so fluently.

Over the next four days, people arrived from the upriver villages. Each village had its own campgrounds, and those were further separated into clan areas. Everyone mingled and told stories of great hunts and feasts. The groups from the western fringes of the river basin told of clashes with the Haudenosaunee. The stories told were about the Long Lake Haudenosaunee people pushing out their river valley relatives from the west and those people pushing the western edges of the lands occupied by the People of the Great River, the *Muhhekekuneuw.*

The fifth day following Broken Bow's arrival marked the first of the three days of the Solstice Celebration. The stickball game on that day left Yellow Hair with a few cuts, many bruises, and more sore muscles than he could count. A long session in the sweat lodge with Bright Moon made him feel better. He was not sure if it was her presence, her special touch, or her applying a mixture of bear grease, mint, and ground willow bark that eased his pain.

She played the next day. She learned quickly that she had no trouble catching the small ball in her net stick, and she could avoid contact from the opposing players while she advanced toward the goal. She found, however, that she lacked the accuracy in throwing the ball needed to get it into the goal. After a few misses, she gave up and flipped the ball toward one of Tall Woman's daughters who was coming up behind her. Cedar Shadow scooped the ball up and put it into the goal. That strategy worked for a few goals until one of the Shodac players ambushed Bright Moon after she caught a pass from Cedar Shadow. She had just turned toward the goal when a woman named Lark cut her legs out from under her. The contact sprained Bright Moon's ankle again, and she was out of the games. This sprain was not as serious as the first time, and she was able to put some weight on it. She found relief in the sweat lodge later with Yellow Hair's ministrations. She would be limping for several days, but his touch always made her forget her pain temporarily.

Broken Bow fashioned her a crutch as a gift. The look in his eye when he handed it to her said that one day he would expect a special payment. She almost refused, but realized how much she needed it, and how much they depended on him to get them to Yellow Hair's people. *Wolf said it would not be easy,* she told herself.

Two mornings after the third and final day of the Solstice they had their canoes loaded and were saying their goodbyes. "My heart will feel a great pain not knowing your fate among those northern wild men." Tall Woman put her worried eyes on Bright Moon.

"Broken Bow says that he will see us to the great canoe of Yellow Hair's people. He will bring word back to you that we have found who we are looking for. My heart will sing whenever I think of you and the kindness you showered on a couple of strangers to whom you owed nothing." They hugged and wiped a tear.

"Long Cat, you have faithfully brought us closer to our destination than we ever dreamed. I have no way to repay you for your service." Yellow Hair placed a strong hand on Long Cat's shoulder.

"It has been my pleasure, Yellow Hair. Your stories are payment aplenty for what little I have done. And your premonition about the dead war chief saved us all from having our hearts and livers eaten. I am the one who owes you. No, I have many stories to tell well into my old age now. I may settle down myself when I get back to Lenape Town. Thankfully it is mostly downstream all the way there. My old arms are feeling their age. Blue Deer will earn his keep on that portage up above." Long Cat tried not to show the moisture in his eyes. He slapped Yellow Hair on the back and gave Bright Moon a long, tight hug.

"I will dearly miss you, friend, and Blue Deer,

you have a great teacher and friend in this one. Thank you for all your help."

Long Cat and Blue Deer started their hard paddle against the current of Cold Water Creek while Yellow Hair and Broken Bow eased into the creek for the short downstream span until they reached the Great River. They would take it to the northern limit of the lands occupied by the People of the Great River. They would soon be out of the lands where they knew they had friends.

CHAPTER 9
MUHHEKUNEUW

As the sun lay low in the western sky on the third day after leaving Cold Water Creek Village, Broken Bow guided them into a small creek channel on the east side. "I see no firepit smoke, why do we stop here? Is there a village nearby?" Yellow Hair questioned Broken Bow.

"No, there is no village near here on the east shore. There are some villages two and four days north on the west side, but my brethren may be making trouble against them, and I would keep you two out of those problems if I could. The hunting is good in these woods, and I thought we could use a day off the water—hunting, fishing, resting. We could use some fresh meat."

Yellow Hair and Bright Moon looked at each

other quizzically. They had traveled farther and faster many times in the past than they were moving now. *Perhaps caution is more important on this river,* Yellow Hair mused to himself.

The next morning, Broken Bow and Yellow Hair left to hunt before the sun broke over the eastern hills, which were becoming noticeably higher. The days were still getting hotter, and the air was still oppressively humid, and it was still early summer.

BRIGHT MOON WAS LOOKING FORWARD to the cooler northern air she had been told about. She could not remember it ever being this hot so early in the summer. She puttered around the campsite, playing with Acorn, mending some worn clothing, and just relaxing. Midmorning Acorn decided he needed a nap and plopped down in the sleeping skins. Bright Moon took the opportunity to put out a fishing line with some venison jerky for bait on a few bone hooks.

Before long, she was hauling in two channel catfish as long as her arm. She had one gutted and was just starting on the second when she heard footsteps coming up the trail. She jumped up to see Broken Bow walking up nonchalantly.

"It seems even the fish are attracted to the young maiden!" He chortled. He never properly referred to her as a "maid," despite her being married with a child and another on the way.

"What are you doing here? I thought you were hunting with Yellow Hair." Bright Moon looked suspiciously at Broken Bow, the bloody obsidian knife still in her hand in a defensive position. Her instincts had warned her that Broken Bow may cause trouble.

"He is trying to stalk a black-colored deer he saw. Very unusual. He correctly says the hide will bring a great price in the northland. I let him stalk the deer. He could do that better by himself. I chased some turkeys that started coming this way, then flushed over a hill. I was close and decided to come here to see if there was any service I could provide you. I see the boy is sleeping. The timing could not be better." He gave her his best seductive smile.

"No matter what the timing is, I will not share my blankets with you."

"You know, Bright Moon, it is the customary among most people I have met in my wide travels, that when a woman travels in the company of two men, she shares her blankets with both. It makes for a smoother trip for all." Broken Bow held his seducing smile pointed at her face.

"Let me make something perfectly clear." She bore her most serious eyes into his as she spoke calmly, "If the Creator himself stood where you are standing and said, 'Bright Moon, I will share your blanket now.' I would tell him, 'Great Spirit, I am married to Yellow Hair. I will share my blankets with no other.' You are being paid to guide us so that we may find Yellow Hair's people. No more than that. We can be friends, and I will forget about your forwardness. But if you press your desires on me, I will kill you, and we will find our way somehow without you. Am I clear on this? Do you understand?"

"All right. Don't get all uppity. I will leave you alone. You can't blame me for trying. I have found most women are attracted to me. If you are not, so be it. But hear this—you will change your mind somewhere along the way, and I will be ready for you. And when you come around, my services will no longer be free." He spoke back to her with an air of confidence.

"I will take that chance. Now you had better go see if you can find those turkeys. I will take care of these fish." She still held the knife in a defensive position, twirling her wrist so that the sun danced and reflected off the bloody blade. He turned and went back up the trail without another word.

Before the sun set, she was playing a hiding

game with Acorn. She had three racks of fish drying over a smoky fire and a fish and arrowhead root stew going. She heard Yellow Hair struggling along the trail, carrying his prized deer. Its fur was black as charcoal. It was a big buck, antlers still in velvet and not yet fully developed. The soft, fuzzy covering over the growing antlers was as black as the fur. He laid the carcass down in the grass next to the campsite and stood huffing and puffing, hands over his head, trying to get his breath back.

Gasping, he finally got out, "That was a long chase...uff...uff...uff...and a longer carry back here." He looked around. "Where is Broken Bow? He should have been back hands of time ago."

"I kind of sent him away for the afternoon. He came back here right after I hauled those fish ashore. He wanted more than just a cup of tea. I told him that would not be happening, that he is being paid to guide us to your people, no more. We reached an understanding...when I told him I would kill him if he pressed the issue. Then I sent him back out hunting. He claimed he was following some turkeys. I told him he had better get back out there and find them. Perhaps they were hard to find."

"You did the right thing. If he has other ideas, we can get along without him somehow. I had better get that deer hung and skinned. You can cut it up after I skin it. That black pelt will be a valuable trade item. I have never seen a deer that black."

"I do not think anyone has. I will need the brain to tan it properly. We will be here another day. Perhaps that fur would make a fine shawl for you?"

"Or you."

Just as the sun slid beyond the mountains west of the Great River, they heard Broken Bow coming down a game trail toward their small camp. When he came into view, he was carrying a large turkey. "I found them!" He held the bird up triumphantly. "And I see you found your black deer. And that stew smells delicious. I am starved!" He acted as if the incident in the morning never happened.

"We will need to stay here another day while Bright Moon tans the deer hide. At least we have plenty of meat."

"So, it would seem. There is a small village on this side of the river about a day north of here. They would have little to trade, but they might appreciate some meat for passage through their lands," Broken Bow said, and began skinning the turkey. He observed that Bright Moon was busy butchering the deer while Yellow Hair staked the skin out on the ground for scraping. Acorn was under foot drawing circles in the bloody dust as

Bright Moon cut strips of meat and placed them on a hastily made rack to dry. She plucked out an eyeball and gave it to the child to chew on.

After she had the deer cut up, they took a break and ate a hearty meal of the catfish stew she had prepared. She wrapped the deer back straps in cleaned intestines to present as a gift to the Sachem of Mink Creek Village. Once she had the rest of the meat on drying racks, the bladder cleaned and drying, and other soft parts processed, she stripped the hamstring tendons and separated the fibers to dry. Once dried, she would rub fat into them to soften them to make thread and string. Finally, the bones were cleaned, and the useful ones set out for drying. At last, she was ready to crack open the back of the skull and remove the brain for rubbing into the hide for tanning it. By the time she was finished with her part of processing the deer, the half moon was high overhead. Acorn had fallen fast asleep with half of the eyeball jelly smeared down the front of him and much of the rest all over his dirty face and hands.

Broken Bow had finished processing his turkey, with some of the meat roasting on sticks next to the fire and the rest drying on the racks between Bright Moon's deer meat. He too was fast asleep.

Yellow Hair was helping Bright Moon as much as he could but was more in the way than helpful.

Finally, she had told him to just go to sleep long before she was finished. When she was done, she was exhausted, and her breasts were so full they hurt. She had missed feeding Acorn his evening meal. Her breasts were producing less milk each day, with a little one newly started in her womb. But the amount she was still producing built up enough pressure to make her uncomfortable. She could not get settled, and finally went out onto the creekbank and milked herself over the bank enough to relieve the pressure. When she laid back down, she was out before she had laid her head next to Yellow Hair's shoulder.

When she awoke, Yellow Hair was making all sorts of ugly faces as he cleaned the dried eye matter from Acorn's face. Broken Bow was nowhere to be seen, and she soon noticed his canoe was gone as well. "Have we lost him?" She sounded as if she were still half asleep.

"Said he was going upriver to let them know we are coming. He took some of the meat we planned to give them. He said the Sachem is a finicky woman who does not like surprises. I think he just did not want to sit around here all day enjoying the domestic life or the view! He prefers to be on the move. Then he said he would wait for us there. My guess is that, since your rejection, he probably has some 'personal' issues to tend to and probably has some connections in that village." Yellow Hair grinned.

"Men! I am glad I do not have to sit around watching him leering at me like a mountain lion watching a deer coming toward him. I suppose you think you are going to get yours when Acorn goes down for his nap today." She smiled coyly at him, a promise on her face.

"It would not hurt." He looked at her sideways.

By nightfall, they had the dried meat loaded in baskets and everything except their sleeping skins loaded in the canoe. They would leave at first light.

Bright Moon was the first to see the blue smoke rising above the trees east of the river in the middle of the afternoon. In less than a finger of time, three big river canoes with six warriors in each met them from upriver. Bright Moon, in the front of the canoe, and with Acorn strapped to her bare chest nursing, raised her hands palms up to signal friendship. The warriors greeted them in a friendly manner and escorted them around the bend and up a small creek a short distance to a canoe landing.

The first thing Yellow Hair noticed was that this village was located on the first terrace above the floodplain and was not surrounded by a palisade. There were two large longhouses, one bearing a wolf carved on a guardian pole, the other a bear. There was no sign of the familiar turtle and turkey clans. But the people appeared friendly and hospitable.

A woman dressed in a dark-red-dyed doeskin dress greeted them. Her decorations and demeanor told them she was the Sachem. Broken Bow conducted the introductions. Bright Moon noted a half dozen maids paying close attention to every word Broken Bow spoke. *At least I need not worry about him bothering me while we are here. She* smiled inwardly, but then noticed a few of them eyeing Yellow Hair up and down. She instinctively moved close to him as soon as she got out of the canoe and wrapped his arm in hers.

A now familiar night of storytelling with Broken Bow providing the words that Yellow Hair or Bright Moon were unable to express followed the introductions and makeshift feast. They learned that Mink Creek Village was insulated from the conflicts with the Haudenosaunee raiders to the west by the villages on the west bank and tributaries of the Great River. From time to time, they sent warriors to support their friends to the west. A few warriors coaxed Yellow Hair and Bright Moon to demonstrate their fabled skills with the bow and arrow the next day. None walked away laughing.

After two days in Mink Creek Village, Yellow

Hair, Bright Moon, Acorn, and Broken Bow were loaded and paddling upriver toward Shodac, where the Great Sachem of the *Muhhekuneuw* kept her longhouse.

The shadows were getting longer when they slid their canoes onto the landing below Shodac. A group of young warriors, boys, and girls gathered around as they started to unload their belongings and trade goods. In the west, thunder beings were sounding their approach. The air was still very warm and humid. The slow water of Shodac Creek harbored swarms of mosquitoes, adding urgency to the task of packing their supplies up the trail to the village. Just before the throng of warriors, porters, children, and guests passed through the overlapping walls of the palisade, the wind increased dramatically and roared through the nearby trees. Clouds of dust were raised from the packed clay path leading into the village. To everyone's liking, the mosquitoes vanished.

Several longhouses surrounded the central plaza. Each had a sentry post with a carved likeness of a clan symbol. There was a bear, a deer, a turkey, a turtle, a heron, an otter, but the largest longhouse belonged to the Wolf Clan. Standing outside of the main entrance was a woman in a white doeskin dress decorated with beadwork in the shape of a wolf's head on the chest. Just above the fringed bottom hem ran a row of black-dyed wolf tracks. The dress was sleeveless, revealing wrinkled and saggy arms with faded geometric pattern tattoos. The woman's gray hair was braided and wound into a bun on the top of her head held in place with turkey bone pins. Her face was a maze of deep wrinkles. Next to her stood a man about her age dressed in a red sleeveless war shirt, though he looked too old for war. His shirt was decorated with quill chevrons and the head of a wolf dyed on the chest. He had faded wolf tattoos on his temples and a black band from cheek to cheek across his large nose. His thin gray hair was shoulder length and hung loosely from his balding scalp. His face was also deeply wrinkled.

Behind and flanking the old couple were a group of men, women, and children who appeared to be family members. Gathering around in the plaza were throngs of people, including warriors, maids, older children, younger children, and dogs. A group of older men and women bearing insignias of the various clans shouldered up but stayed together. Yellow Hair rightfully guessed these were the Shodac council members.

When all were gathered, Broken Bow proceeded with the formal introductions. He introduced the old woman as Wolf Mother, Great Sachem of all the *Muhhekuneuw*. "We should move into the longhouse now, before the storm is upon us." She had to raise her voice to be heard over the increasing wind. "Put their things along the wall under the shelter. Cover them with some heavy skins to keep them dry," she yelled to the young adults holding the bags and baskets of trade goods.

Storm clouds billowed over the western wall of the palisade. Lightning flashes made the clouds every color imaginable against the background of the darkening sky. The smell of rain was in the air.

Once inside the big room of the longhouse, Wolf Mother told her servants to prepare tea, stew, and cakes for the guests. She indicated for them to sit close to her along the central fire pit. There were no fires because of the heat, but torches lit the room. The smoke holes had been closed against the approaching storm, leaving just enough space for the smoke from the torches to escape. By the time everyone was seated, the thunder beings were all around as the battle raged between them and the underground spirits. Driving rain slammed against the bark walls and roof while the strong winds made every joint of the longhouse creek. By the time everyone was fed, the thunder beings had moved on. The rain continued to fall, but the wind died down considerably.

After the meal, Wolf Mother gave Acorn a

small turtle rattle to play with and told Broken Bow to interpret Yellow Hair and Bright Moon's stories. Yellow Hair was able to get most of his tales related without Broken Bow's help, but Bright Moon needed more assistance. As usual, everyone in the room was amazed at their adventures as they were told.

The old man, Black Coat, War Chief of Shodac and husband to Wolf Mother, was most interested in Yellow Hair's dealings with Ganeco and was awed by Bright Moon's description of her fight with Thunder Throat. "Only in the legends of long ago do we hear such tales of bravery and battle prowess by a woman. But you carry yourself like a warrior. I tend to believe your stories," Black Coat commented.

"She carries herself like a pregnant warrior," Wolf Mother said to Black Coat. "This place you seek, the great canoe of the foreigners...people who would know tell me it takes two moons to get there. Winter will arrive before you do. Those foreigners will be gone before you make it there. What will you do? Where will you stay?" she asked Yellow Hair.

"We have been delayed too many times. I had hoped we would reach them this season, but now you tell me it cannot be done." Yellow Hair looked sheepishly at Bright Moon.

Broken Bow spoke up. "I have friends at the end of the Mouth River where it flows into the Great River to the Morning Sun. They have canoes that travel very fast to the ocean. I think we can get there before Yellow Hair's people leave for the winter."

"Very well, we will not detain you here."

"We have gifts for all who help us on our journey, Great Sachem." Yellow Hair gave the old woman a deferential bow of his head.

"Nonsense! You are my guests. You need pay no tribute here. The flesh eaters you encounter further north will take all you own, I fear."

The morning broke with a clear sky, lower humidity, and refreshing temperatures. They were on the water before the sun broke over the eastern mountains.

CHAPTER 10

THE LAST RIVER

Ten days after leaving Shodac, they arrived at Mouth River Village. They had hurried down the length of Mouth of the Country Lake to the Mouth River and followed it to its confluence with the Great River That Flows to the Morning Sun. They avoided contact with the fishermen on the lake and only spoke briefly with warriors they encountered. Broken Bow knew everyone, and they let him pass unheeded. Bright Moon was happy to have Acorn clinging to her, and now her belly carried a small bump that showed she was with child, so she did not have to endure the want in every young warrior's eyes. Now they looked right past her and focused on Yellow Hair's light-colored head.

After formal introductions, Broken Bow spoke

directly to the head matron, Salmon Heart. "We are in a desperate hurry to reach the bay where the foreign great canoe comes each year. We will need two of your big canoes and strong warriors to paddle them. It is most important that we get there before the foreigners leave for the winter."

"You may be in luck," Salmon Heart began. "The great canoe arrived late this summer, I am told. The Micmac in that bay had hoped the foreign traders had abandoned them. As it turns out they were just delayed for some reason known only to them. One of those great canoes sailed past here last summer. They must have run into trouble, for when they returned down river, most of their warriors were wrapped in bloody rags and part of their canoe had charred wood showing. Also, it seemed there were not as many of them. Most of their kind only cause problems. The traders who come to visit the Micmac seem to be an exception...IF you can trust what the Micmac say. They are an unreliable source. I wish these two luck going among them."

"Yellow Hair here, is one of the foreigners, obviously. He needs to get back to his people, and Bright Moon will go where her husband goes. My job is to get them there before his people leave." Broken Bow pointed to the couple. Yellow Hair and

Bright Moon could only catch the meaning of an occasional word or phrase.

"What have you to offer for the use of these warriors and their canoes, trader?" Salmon Heart looked hard at Broken Bow.

Broken Bow turned to Yellow Hair and said, "She wants to know what you have to pay for the warriors and canoes."

Yellow Hair went to his packs and pulled out three bags. One was much heavier than the other two. "Offer her this bag of shell beads worked by masters in Cahokia, this bag of gorgets, and this bag of copper nuggets from north of the Grandfather River."

"That seems like a lot. Are you sure?" Broken Bow asked.

"Yes. It will be worth it if they get us there on time."

Broken Bow showed Salmon Heart the goods. Those watching gasped in awe at the beautifully carved and painted gorgets.

Salmon Heart looked at Broken Bow with iron in her dark eyes. Then she looked hard at Yellow Hair. She picked up two of the copper nuggets and scraped them together, assessing their quality. She ran her hand through the shell beads.

"The shells are from the great Southern Ocean.

Yellow Hair acquired them in the great city of Cahokia on the Grandfather River."

Without acknowledging, Salmon Heart picked up a painted gorget. Her focus turned from hard glare to mild skepticism. It depicted Turtle Island with the Tree of Life rising from its back. Eagle, falcon, raven, hawk, and a thunderbird circled around the tree. An owl sat on a branch. A wolf, a deer, a bear, and a beaver stood at the base of the tree on the turtle's back. A coyote slunk in the background. Horned Serpent and Water Panther entwined in the turtle's legs. She stared at it several heartbeats, then slipped it into a pouch on her waist belt. She looked at Bright Moon and gave a quick half-smile, then turned to Yellow Hair and nodded. He put his right vertical fist in his left upturned palm and gave a small jerk, the universal trader's gesture meaning "good trade."

Salmon Heart then called for a feast. Her longhouse was not nearly as big as others they were used to, but they were made welcome for the night. After a hearty meal of fish stew and rice cakes flavored with blueberries, they sat by the fire, and the travelers related their usual tales of adventure, near deaths, and all they had been through. Salmon Heart was intrigued by their descriptions of Cahokia. She had never talked to someone who had actually seen it with their own eyes.

Salmon Heart, through Broken Bow as interpreter, introduced Yellow Hair to her son, Salmon Eye. He would lead their group to the land of the Micmac. "You must do as I say," Salmon Eye began. "The Micmac people can be very difficult. We have been at war with them as long as our memories have been spoken. They often hunt our moose and caribou and have been known to take our children and women as slaves. We will need to be very careful around them. Is that understood?"

"Yes, I understand. For my part, I want you to introduce me to the Micmac as 'Tor Eriksson.' Can you say that?" Yellow Hair asked. Broken Bow had to try several times before he was able to say it to Yellow Hair's satisfaction.

"Why would you change your name for the Micmac?" Salmon Eye asked.

"I need to start using the name given by my people—the Norse. They will need to know who I am before I can convince them to take me back to Greenland. Once they understand who I am, I will be welcome among them."

"And what of your woman? Will you leave her among the Micmac?" Salmon Eye was studying Bright Moon from head to toe.

"Bright Moon is my wife. She will go where I go, and you and your men will stay away from her. She will be introduced as '*Heidr Tungl,*' the Norse words for Bright Moon. And my son's name is *Erik* from this time on. He is no longer to be called Acorn."

"You have paid a high price for me and my warriors to take you through very dangerous lands. And it is not just the Micmac you need to be fearful of...the weather can be unpredictable and dangerous; bears and moose can easily kill a man who is not vigilant or a woman and small boy. I will get you there, but you must always do as I say. Do we understand one another, *Dtor Arreeksaan?*"

"Yes."

As the sun was coming up the next morning, they were loading their bags and baskets into two large, high sided river canoes. Broken Bow joined nine warriors in one while Tor took a paddling position in the other. Bright Moon and Acorn, now Heidr Tungl and Erik, sat on a bag of sleeping skins next to Tor on the floor. She still nursed her son, though her milk had nearly disappeared because she was pregnant again, but he was now walking and difficult to keep close to her. She tied a cord around his waist so he could not wander far enough to interfere with the other canoe paddlers.

Immediately after they entered the big river, a

mass of islands appeared before them. Rapids roiled and tossed in the most visible channels. Tor expected they would be pulling into the shore and portaging the heavy canoes past the rapids. Instead, the warriors steered the canoes to one of the channels where the rapids were not as fearsome as most of the other channels. Once in the fast-moving water, there was no turning back, but the warriors guided them through without incident. At first, Erik became frightened by the roaring water, the speed they were moving, and the jostling around, but soon he saw it as fun and giggled. They quickly cleared the rapids but were still in a fast-moving section of the river and sped rapidly to the east.

A few of the warriors were from a village on the south bank of the river just below the rapids. Because of the clan ties between the villages, there was no need to stop at this village. After that, Tor was surprised at how few people they encountered as they sped downriver. At the start of the second day, Broken Bow traded places with the warrior just behind Tor so they could talk about what lay ahead. The first day Broken Bow had gleaned as much information from the warriors around him as he could. He had never been east of Mouth River Village.

"We will be traveling through lands controlled

by the real people for many days. There are few villages and no great towns all the way to the bay where your people anchor their great canoe. In four days, we will come to another set of rapids. Below those rapids, the river becomes salty like the sea and begins to widen. From that point on we will be subject to bigger waves, and the water rises and falls with the moon. When the water recedes toward the open ocean, we can move faster. And when the water is rising, it will be like paddling upriver. A couple of days after reaching the salty water, we will no longer be able to see the north shoreline. If the seas are relatively calm, we will reach the bay in ten-and-two days. If we face storms or if the waves are too big to navigate, we will need to stay on shore until the big waves pass.

"In a hand of days, we will enter the land of the Micmac people. They can be difficult but will prob-ably be happy to accept some of your exotic beads and colored stones to let us pass through to the bay. They like to make their arrow points from the hard, green stones. They have sources to get stones like that, but I am sure they will like yours as well. Where in your travels did they come from? I have to say that calling you *Dtor Arreeksaan* is difficult after calling you 'Yellow Hair' all this time."

"Tor is the name given me by my mother and

father. 'Yellow Hair' was given by the Lenape when I passed into manhood. Now that I may be going back to my people, I think I need to use my old name, and my son is named after my father. There are sources for the green stones in the lands of Bright Moon's people. But it seems some of your relatives, what we call the *Minquas*, have decided that they need to control the trade of those rocks, so they are getting harder to come by. To me, the shiny black rocks are more valuable. They are easier to work to a very sharp point that stays sharp a long time."

"Where does that rock come from? I have traded it for as long as I can remember but have never seen any place where it is dug up."

"I have never seen it mined either, but Traveler told me it comes from the Shining Mountains far to the west across the great grasslands. At one time, I thought I might want to see those mountains, but Cahokia is as far as I got," Tor answered, a bit of melancholy in his voice.

"I have heard your stories and see that you seem to be at home wherever you are. Why is it so important to return to your ancestral lands?"

"Not sure that I can answer that...some longing in my heart. Also, I feel like I can open a trade system between the people of Turtle Island and those of my homeland. My people need to be educated about the riches that can be exchanged between the two worlds."

"The warrior I talked with yesterday, Barbed Bone, tells me that the trade between your people and the Micmac is about worn out. Your people demand much and give little in return. And they have made enemies with just about every other people they have encountered. That great canoe Salmon Heart talked about tried to force their way past some of my Haudenosaunee relatives at the mouth of the great inland freshwater sea we call *The Great Shining Water*. Our people greatly outnumbered them and nearly burned their great canoe. They were lucky that any survived. If you bring people like that back here, they will be most unwelcome, I am sure. I hope more of your people are like you."

"Yes, my people need to be educated in manners. But I must say that I have witnessed some harsh cruelties in my travels on Turtle Island as well. The hearts of too many men are dark. If I am able, I will shed light in as many hearts as I can," Tor reflected, resolution in his tone.

"You are a good man. I wish you the best. I saw this darkness you speak of at an early age. The only man I knew who did not carry the weight of hate in his heart was an old trader who used to visit our village once a sun cycle. When I had seen ten-and-two summers and he came to my village, I packed up and went with him. He took me under his wing and taught me the trade life, and I have never looked back. I can go among most peoples and not be concerned about their trivial blood feuds." Broken Bow made no attempt to hide his pride.

"You are a good man, too. If you have a fault, it would be your wandering eye." Tor turned to show the sincerity in his words. Bright Moon turned to Tor half smiling, half blushing. After a pause, Tor looked at Bright Moon and winked. "It could get you in trouble."

"Yes, well, I am who I am. Most women welcome my advances...and many make the advances. It comes easy for me, and I see no reason to ignore the talents the gods have bestowed on me."

Bright Moon turned and pretended to play with Erik. She would let Tor handle this.

"Well, you are your own man, just be careful... you could wake up dead one of these days." Tor smiled and went back to his paddling.

"You know how hard it is for me to call you 'Tor,' don't you? I have only known you as 'Yellow Hair' since we met. It is like using a stranger's name," Bright Moon offered when they had a moment alone. "And calling 'Acorn,' 'Eereek' is so strange. I hope I can get used to it before we meet your people."

"You will. You always do more than you think you can. I will teach you as much of the Norse tongue as I can while we travel...at least what I can remember." Tor tried to sound confident.

CHAPTER 11

MICMAC LANDS

They encountered only a few villages along the river, and the experienced warriors guided the big canoes through the last rapids into the salt water with no problems. Each day during the last hand of time before landing at a campsite, the warriors at the rear of the canoes would stretch a net between the two canoes. They nearly always brought up enough fish for a stew or roasting the meat on sticks. Doing this, they did not have to dip into their supplies of pemmican and jerked venison. Tor learned that turkeys did not live this far north, but everyday moose and deer appeared along the river. The warriors said they would not take the time to kill a moose unless they ran out of food. Killing a moose would delay them at least a couple of days while the meat would be drying and the hide curing.

Barbed Bone hailed Broken Bow and announced they had passed into Micmac lands. The landmark Barbed Bone used to determine that was unknown and unnoticed by Broken Bow and Tor.

The coast to their right was mostly straight and unremarkable. Sandy beach gave way to gravel and a rocky rise that soon flattened into a plain of scrub brush and eventually taller trees and higher hills. All that could be made out on the north shore was a hazy line of green mixing with the blue of the seawater. Past the shoreline, clouds hung like they may have been associated with higher land. It was difficult to see that far. For three days, they were blessed with calm seas, clear skies, and warm weather.

At each creek or small river emptying into the salt water, they encountered groups of fishermen. They occupied small temporary camps along the creeks near the mouths. The camps consisted of a few conical skin tents in loose clusters. Usually, one of the tents was bigger than the others, and it belonged to their chief. They fished with nets from small canoes. Women and children scoured the water's edge for the plentiful shellfish.

Most days they passed the fish camps with

Salmon Eye holding up his oversized, white-painted arrow with white fletching and a dull wooden point, indicating he came in peace. The fish camps had no desire for trouble, so they exchanged greetings and let them pass unhindered. Late one evening they came to a camp and set up their tents just outside the temporary village. They watched the warriors at work catching fish.

After dark, three men set out in a canoe. The man in the middle would maneuver the canoe with his paddle. Tied to the side of the canoe, an upright stick held a frayed birch wood torch that had been dipped in birch oil. The torch hung over the side of the canoe so that the light would attract the plentiful cod. A man with a spear stood on either side of the paddler. They speared fish after fish while the torch lasted. When the torch burned out, they brought their haul ashore, fashioned a new torch, and went back out for more fish. The spear fishing went on as long as the cod were running close to shore.

Their spears had three points. The outside points were made from moose leg bones and shaped to a dull point. The outside edge was smooth, and the inner flared to a ridge, then tapered back to where it was fastened to the spear handle. Two of those points were fastened so that the ridges faced one another with a shorter leg bone sharpened to a chisel point placed between them. The sharpened point was set just inside the outside points where they tapered back toward the handle. The spear was thrust into the fish, the sharpened point piercing the body and the outside points sliding around and gripping the fish so that it could not slide off the sharpened point.

Their unusual canoes were about twice as long as a man is tall and made from a birch wood frame and covered with birch bark. The front and back were rounded and covered to almost a leg length with the bark skin, giving protection from the waves washing over the front and rear. The centers of the gunwales were raised a couple of hands high and tapered down to the normal gunwale height before turning up again front and back.

The women butchered the fish and hung strips of the meat on wooden racks made from driftwood or willow saplings. Some of the entrails were used for bait on hooks the women set out in the creek to catch trout.

They left the fish camp the next morning and continued east. Two days later, they woke up as the sky began to lighten and found themselves shrouded in a dense fog. The air smelled salty and felt cold. As it grew lighter, all they saw was fog. Everything outside their tents was covered in dripping wetness. Their driftwood fire hissed as the wood cracked and sent sparks into the misty sky. Soon enough, Bright Moon had what was left of last night's catch warmed up and some willow tea spiced with some berries she found ready for the warriors to get their day started. Tor wondered if they could travel in this fog. He remembered the look and smell of a fog like this when they were lost at sea in his father's broken ship. It seemed like many lifetimes past.

Despite the fog, the warriors were breaking camp and loading the canoes. The sea was nearly dead calm, but the tide was going out, and they were soon sliding along the coast to the east. All day long, the sun was but a bright spot in a gray world. It was difficult to even tell up from down. Occasionally a gull or two could be heard calling through the mist, but for the most part, the only sound all day long was the paddles stroking the water, the shushing of the canoes through the water, and intermittent low murmuring of quiet conversation. The quiet was interrupted at times by the laughter or crying of a sandy-haired little boy who was bored and scared. On two occasions, they passed creeks entering the salt water. They could hear people talking, but no alarms were raised, so they just kept paddling eastward.

When it was obvious the light was failing, they

found a small stream to camp by for the night. The stream was too small to attract a temporary village and cod fisherman but did provide them with a source of fresh water. The following day was a repeat of the day before. The east wind was barely noticeable, and their lives remained shrouded in fog. Just before the weak sunlight began to disappear, a few blue patches drifted overhead, the easterly breeze picked up, and the waves began to grow. They found a suitable campsite in a small cove and pulled ashore. Driftwood was plentiful in the cove, but so were biting black flies. The flies forced them to move away from the cove to a less protected beach where the wind kept the flies grounded.

The next day they were forced to stay in camp because strong easterly winds built the waves too high to negotiate with their canoes. After a day in camp, they were anxious to get moving again and were rewarded with a shift to light southeast breezes. The seas were calm, and they made good time. The change was so gradual that they barely noticed the land curving away to the southeast. They encountered a few more fish camps and were regarded cautiously, but no problems arose.

Heidr Tungl hated it when they were forced to stay in camp all day. It meant that all day long she would have to endure Broken Bow leering at her with want in his eyes. Every time Tor was out of hearing range, Broken Bow would make joking remarks about how it had been so long since he had a woman to warm his blankets. She was tempted to use her war club on him. He cleverly always acted helpful and friendly whenever Tor was around, so she knew it would do no good to complain and understood the ramifications if she permanently silenced Broken Bow. His forwardness only abated slightly as her belly grew.

Three days later the coast was noticeably bending to the southeast. The fish camps were getting larger and less friendly. A sort of guarded tolerance was how Tor thought of their treatment by the Micmac people. He had saved a few shell beads, and the women seemed happy to get them. He listened with eager enthusiasm as a group of fishermen described the great canoe with what looked like a square wing from some unknown great bird. The Micmac fishermen told them if they continued to follow the coast, it would curve around to a bay where the canoe was resting in the shallow water.

Their chief had negotiated to let the men cut a certain number of trees. Even now some men were off in the forest cutting big trees with terrible axes while others dragged the fallen trees to the water's edge. Some trees took days to slide overland behind two large animals that did as the men bid. The animals pulled the logs to the small river in which the trees could be floated to the bay where the great canoe lay. Tor could not get enough of this information. He knew the ship would still be there when they arrived. One of the older boys in the big fish camp offered to ride in a canoe to guide them to the great canoe. Salmon Eye reluctantly allowed the boy, whose name was Blue Jay, to come along. If nothing else, he might be useful as a hostage.

Blue Jay wore a big smile on his face while he constantly and enthusiastically asked questions. He had a way of ingratiating many of the warriors around him. He settled in next to Heidr Tungl and Erik. The child took to him instantly, laughing and giggling while Blue Jay played hide his face and pop-up games with him. After a while, Blue Jay pulled out a piece of old bowstring from his waist belt pouch and wowed Erik by making shaped nets in his fingers. Heidr Tungl recalled her mother teaching her and her sister those shapes. That seemed like an eternity past. A hot tear trickled down her cheek. Tor noted the faraway look in her eye, rested his paddle, and put his arm around her briefly. She smiled a "thank you" to him.

After following the coast curving more to a southerly direction all day, suddenly it gently turned east-southeast again and went far out into the sea. Tor had been getting weary and tired of paddling. Now he was depressed. *How far does this coast go?* he wondered to himself. Salmon Eye guided them to the beach where a small creek interrupted the shoreline's wide curve as it changed directions. Blue Jay was jubilant. "Before the sun sets tomorrow, we will see the great canoe!" he exclaimed as they unloaded the canoes.

"You can treaty with the Micmac chief, Salmon Eye, but I need to talk to the Norse chief myself," Tor said to the man emphatically, looking him in the eye.

"Of that, I have no doubt," Salmon Eye replied, then added, "I have no need nor desire to talk to a man I will not understand...and will probably dislike as much as he dislikes me. I hope we have no war because he accuses me of kidnapping you."

"You have already talked to our chief, Salmon Eye. Only a few men and women are left in our village to cook for the chief of the foreigners," Blue Jay interrupted. He knew his father was already paddling up a creek that would get him to their home village before these travelers would arrive.

"I will explain everything to him so you can get headed back west. You have a long return trip. I hope it is as uneventful as the trip over here."

"It won't be…the weather has been too favorable for too long."

"In any case, I thank you for bringing us here. You and your warriors have been most helpful." Tor tried to sound friendly. His mind was racing. His mouth was so unaccustomed to speaking Norse, he would probably be tongue-tied. *Will I even be able to make the words? Will I even know the words?* He could feel a sleepless night coming.

Tor could see that the sun was rising over land far to the east. Salmon Eye said there was a large island out there and beyond that, an even larger island where the seal hunters make their camps. Blue Jay piped up. "Sometimes our hunters cross the water to that island and hunt seals as well. I do not care for the strong, fishy taste of the meat, but the oil from their fat makes our lamps glow warm all winter."

Salmon Eye was growing tired of Blue Jay's always interrupting conversations between the men. "Do the Micmac have no manners? Did no one ever tell you it is not polite for boys to interrupt their elders all the time?" Salmon Eye growled at Blue Jay.

"I am just being helpful," Blue Jay replied jovially and went to play with Erik. Erik could now walk and followed Blue Jay around the camp like a puppy while Heidr Tungl warmed up a fish and clam stew and some willow tea.

While Blue Jay was playing with Erik, Tor and Heidr Tungl went to the stream, stripped, and bathed in the cold water. He wanted his skin clean and pure on this day. After getting out, he used his fingers to stream his shoulder-blade-length hair out to its fullest. He wanted the Norsemen to see a full head of yellow hair approaching. When they got close, he would be in the front of the canoe for his countrymen to see who was coming. He would hold the arrow of peace high—he wanted no mistakes. He wore his plain brown tanned hunting shirt and brown leggings but insisted that Heidr Tungl be dressed in her finest. He soon found out, however, that her finest dress no longer fit over her expanding belly. So, she also wore her plain brown dress that had been made to fit her right up to midwinter when the baby would be born. But he brought out a white fox skin shoulder wrap and had her wear her hair up in a bun held in place with copper pins.

The sun was already a finger above the horizon when they shoved off. The day started chilly but promised to warm up with a slight southern breeze and sunny sky. Blue Jay's constant chattering, mostly aimed at Erik now, put Heidr Tungl in a happy mood, but she could see the tension building in Tor's body.

She spoke in the Monongahela dialect so only he would understand, "What is it, husband? You seem afraid to meet your own people."

"I...I am worried that I won't remember their tongue well enough. Will I even be able to speak to them? What if they see us as enemies and kill us? Maybe I should go alone to their camp while you and Erik stay back out of sight." All confidence was gone from his voice.

"You have been away from them a long time, but not a lifetime. They will quickly see you as the great man you are and embrace you fully. You have been talking the words to me. They will hear your words of peace, too. If they do not, I will kill every one of them," she said with a wide, devilish smile. He just smiled back and dug his paddle into the water with renewed vigor.

CHAPTER 12
THORKELL'S SHIP

A hand and two fingers of time passed while they paddled along the northeast side of the spit of land. Tor could not see over the ridge running parallel to the shore but noticed gulls constantly circling and looping through the trees along the southwestern skyline. The land ended abruptly, and before Tor realized it, they were moving northwest along the spit of land they had been following to the southeast. The breeze and low waves pushed them rapidly along the shore. There was no beach on this side, only a rocky shoreline. They followed that shoreline for what seemed like an eternity to Tor.

Gradually the shore bent to the west. From the haze, Tor could tell land was just over the horizon to the southwest. A few irregularities in the shoreline began to show up as they pushed farther west. As the morning turned to afternoon, it became evident they were in a bay and moving into the head of it. The southwestern shore slowly came into view, along with small islands and spits of land. Finally, the bay divided, and Blue Jay indicated they should follow the north shore up the bay on their right side. As the bay narrowed and they rounded a gentle curve in the shoreline, ahead near the beach, Tor spotted Thorkell's ship.

Tor could not hold back the tears when he saw Thorkell's banner flapping in the breeze at the top of the mast. Now Heidr Tungl wrapped an arm around his back and hugged him. No words were spoken.

Tor told Salmon Eye to pull to the shore well beyond arrow range from the ship. So far, no Norse or Micmac had been seen, and apparently, they had not been seen by anyone. *Too quiet!* Tor thought. *They may have an ambush set up.* He quietly told Salmon Eye he would proceed alone. Blue Jay piped up, "Tor, my friend, you need me to interpret for you. Your Micmac is not that good. Besides, they know me—no harm will come if I am with you." He had a disarming way about him that sounded convincing.

Then Heidr Tungl spoke up. "They will not harm a pregnant woman or a child. Erik, come with us." She picked him up and defiantly turned to Tor.

"Salmon Eye, how about the rest of you stay with the canoes and flee if trouble starts? There is no need for you to get mixed up in a Norse misunderstanding."

"We will wait here and see what happens."

"I do not suppose there is any point in asking if I can join you?" Broken Bow asked.

"No. The fewer voices, the fewer chances of something going wrong," Tor replied.

When they turned to walk down the beach, they could see a few thin tendrils of smoke rising from the forest beyond the Norse ship. Tor proceeded cautiously, holding the big white arrow over his head.

Before they were in bow range, shouts went up, both in Norse and in Micmac, alerting everyone that strangers approached. Tor was surprised they had gotten that close. From the forest to the north of the ship stepped ten Micmac warriors dressed in tan war shirts carrying strung bows with nocked arrows. From around the bow end of the ship came fifteen Norsemen in full battle gear. Each wore heavy leather war tunics with thick shingles of ox hide cascading down from the shoulders. Each man carried a round shield painted black and red with a black metal boss in the center. A battle axe was carried by each warrior.

A big man in the middle took a step out in front of the others. He stopped, and the others stopped behind him. He was the first man that Heidr Tungl had ever seen who was bigger than Thunder Throat. His shoulder-length hair was orange with streaks of gray. A shiny gold ring adorned each ear. He was missing a couple of front teeth, and his face was covered with long gray hair with some orange patches in it. It looked like the face of some hideous dog, but she could see that he was a powerful man. She hoped her war club would not be needed. It looked like it would bounce harmlessly off him, no matter where she struck. The Micmac warriors stayed to the forest side of the beach. They were now only about fifty paces apart. Tor lowered the arrow and held it out, palms up. The Micmac talked quietly among themselves but stayed ready for any tricks.

The big Norse warrior spoke first. "In the name of the Lord, who comes to this beach?" he shouted slowly in Norse.

"I am Tor Eriksson, I come in peace!" Tor called back, his Norse rusty and projected with an odd accent.

"Tor Eriksson, we have been waiting for you! Tell your friends back there to come forth without their bows. They stand no chance against us. If you are here in peace, as the chief has told us, you have nothing to fear. I want to hear what this is all about, so get them over here, and we will talk," the big man said, leaving no room for questions.

Tor turned and saw Salmon Eye's men all had their bows strung and arrows knocked. Tor turned to the big Norseman and yelled, "I am sending this boy back to tell them to leave their weapons." He pointed to Blue Jay.

"So be it. Be sure there are no tricks!"

Blue Jay ran back to the canoes and talked with Salmon Eye for several heartbeats. Salmon Eye looked at Tor for any other signal. Tor held the arrow toward Salmon Eye, palms up, then turned slowly toward the Norsemen. Salmon Eye turned to his men, and they began to unstring their bows and set them into the canoes. Then they approached cautiously. Tor and Heidr Tungl slowly walked toward the Norsemen. He heard the big man say "Peace!" in Micmac toward the warriors at the forest edge. They slowly relaxed their bows but did not unstring them.

When Salmon Eye and his men stood close behind Tor, he said, "Who is the master of this Norse ship?"

The big man chuckled. Tor did not know if it was because his Norse was so poor, or if the man thought it funny for him to ask a question. "Bjarni Einarrson of Borg, in Iceland. I am master on this ship, but it belongs to another man in Iceland. Now, Tor Eriksson, if that is who you claim to be, who are you and from where do you hail? To my knowledge, and I have been coming to these lands for more than five years, there are no Norse settlements in these parts. So, who are you?"

"As I stated, my name is Tor Eriksson. My uncle, or I should say, my great-uncle is Thorkell Rolfcarlson of the Western Settlements of Greenland. I see by the banner that this is his ship. More than ten years past, my father, Erik Haraldson, and his cousin, Olaf Haakonson, and all our households set out from Ulfrstadt, Norway, for Greenland in two great knorrs. We ran into heavy storms off the coast of Iceland. I know not the fate of Olaf's ship, but my father's ship was slowly broken apart, and I was the only survivor that I am aware of. I washed up on a beach and was rescued by the Lenape people and have traveled these lands extensively until now when I have finally found my own countrymen. The story is longer and very complicated, but here I am. What can you tell me of Thorkell? Does he yet live?" To his surprise, Tor's Norse came flooding back to him. He did not want to stop talking.

"Thorkell lives. He owns this ship. But he no

longer lives in the Western Settlements. He makes his home in Iceland now, near Borg. Will he know Tor Eriksson if he sees him?" Bjarni demanded.

"I know not. I had seen only ten summers when last I was in his presence. Twelve years by my reckoning. Is that correct?" Tor started to confuse himself—too many tongues, too many ways to count and name things.

While Tor and Bjarni bantered back and forth, Salmon Eye started discussions with the Micmac chief. The chief told him they were guests and would be treated with honor while in his village. He confided that the Norsemen would be told they are no longer welcome here and not to come back. They had taken too many trees, and the forest was crying. In addition, their men were taking too many liberties with the Micmac maidens.

Bjarni invited Tor to his camp so that they could finish their discussions in more comfortable conditions. When it became visible, Tor could see Bjarni's tent was huge. It was made up of oiled sailcloth and took up more ground than the lodge of the Micmac chief, Bull Moose.

While they were walking toward the tent, Bjarni asked, "Tor Eriksson, will you tell me who this lovely woman is?"

"Her name is *Heidr Tungl* **Tors**wife. The boy is Erik Torsson, named after my father. He has seen one summer. She carries my second child in her womb." Tor stood tall and straight, looking Bjarni in the eye like an equal.

"Wife, you call her, eh!" Bjarni chuckled. "And where in this endless forest did you find a priest to perform this marriage of yours? You may not know it, but the church forbids the marriage of Christians with heathens. Your 'wife' will only be your whore in Greenland if that is where you intend to go. The same law applies to Iceland, so that matters not. The Skræling have no standing in civilized society. But she is a looker though! I am sure the priest in Brattahlid will not recognize her as anything but a savage, and the two sprats of mixed blood will never have standing. You should have thought about that before you wet your worm."

Tor bristled but held his tongue.

Once inside, there was a circle of chairs around a central fire trough. The ridge of the tent had a smoke hole in the center and vents in each end at the peak so air could flow through. It was not a cold-weather tent—they would not be here much longer. At the end of the fire trough was an intricately carved High Chair reminiscent of the ones Tor remembered from his homeland.

They moved into the tent and took seats where Bjarni indicated. Broken Bow was asked to sit in a chair along with Bjarni's men, and the rest around the room behind the big circle. Broken Bow sat on the ground in front of the chair while everyone else sat in the chairs that were simply pieces of notched logs stood on end, cut so a seat and back were formed. Bull Moose and Salmon Eye did not join them in the Norse tent.

"I want to hear about this *marriage* of yours. Perhaps you have been lost so long, you have no knowledge of the meaning." Bjarni looked at Tor as if he were a wayward child.

"We were married according to the ways and customs of her people. I am sure I can discuss it with the priest. But get this clear right now, Bjarni, these people are not *Skræling*. They are civilized in their own ways and just as much *real* people as any people anywhere. There are many different peoples all across this land. I have traveled over only a portion of it and met only a small number of them. Turtle Island, as they call it, is as vast as all of the Norse world and the ocean combined."

Bjarni chuckled again. "Now I know you have gone daft. Have you hit your head somewhere in your travels? Tell me your story from the start. You are welcome to call them what you wish, but among the Norse, they are Skræling."

Erik began to fuss. Bjarni gave Heidr Tungl an evil eye, so she got up to take him outside. She had understood but few words and was getting rather bored. She also did not like the way Bjarni was talking, or his unwelcomed leering. It was like he was in a higher place than the rest of them. He reminded her of The Great Sun in Cahokia. Yellow Hair tried to stop her, but she convinced him that this was no place for Erik at the moment. When she stepped out the door of the tent, she was surprised that it was already dark. No wonder Erik was fussy, he must be starving.

Suddenly Blue Jay was in her face, smiling of course. He patted Erik on the back, who reacted by twisting away and screeching. "He is hungry," Heidr Tungl said. "Is there a fire where we can find some food?"

"I will take you to my father's lodge." Blue Jay's indomitable cheerful spirit was on full display.

The longhouse was a smaller version of what Bright Moon had known her whole life. It was made of poles covered with bark like she was used to, but it was much lower, not even two times as high as a man is tall. The shape was like that of the Muhhekuneuw, the long side running east and west with the door to the east. The bottom where it joined the ground was banked up to at least knee-high with rocks and covered with earth. The door hanging was made so that it could be closed tight against the brutal cold of the north country winter. Around the village were several more of these small longhouses. Most were closed-up and unoccupied, the residents away at the fish camps. Unlike other villages she had been in, this one seemed to have no formal organization. The longhouse of Bull Moose was a little larger than the others, but unremarkable in any other way. She noted there were no clan markers anywhere. In addition to the longhouses, there were a few of the conical, open-topped tents like she had seen in the fish camps. They sat close to new longhouses that were under construction.

Inside she found caribou and moose hides lining the walls and ceiling up to the single smoke hole. A central fire pit burned low, and it was quite warm inside. Clay pots and skin bags hung close to the fire on tripods. The smells spoke of fish stew and willow tea. Rice and blueberry cakes were laid out and baking on a flat slate slab. The beds were low benches hidden under piles of animal skins. Various bags and baskets along with weapons hung from the walls. A single red and black mask depicting the creator was attached to a support pole just east of the fire pit. Another pole with a slab of bark for a backrest stood west of the fire pit. Bull Moose sat on a pile of skins with his back against the bark backrest casually smoking a plain, gray stone pipe. No partition separated any part of the large room.

"Ah, the Monongahela maid pays us a visit," Bull Moose spoke. Heidr Tungl could not tell if he was welcoming her or telling her she was unwelcome, her understanding of the Micmac tongue was still incomplete.

"I invited her for evening meal, Father. Her son is hungry, and the Norse are not eating yet," Blue Jay offered. A woman stepped up from behind Bull Moose and beckoned her to sit to the left of Bull Moose. From a basket, a younger woman produced carved wooden plates, spoons, and cups. She served Bull Moose, then Blue Jay, then the older woman, Heidr Tungl, and finally, herself. Blue Jay, the old woman, and the younger woman sat, in order, to Bull Moose's right. Blue Jay introduced them as White Goose, Bull Moose's wife and mother to Blue Jay and his sister, Red Doe. Red Doe's husband, Gray Hawk, was away at the fish camp where they met Blue Jay.

With Blue Jay's help, Heidr Tungl introduced herself, using her Norse name, as Tor's wife and Erik as his son. His second child was growing in her belly. White Goose and Red Doe smiled. Red Doe nodded her head and patted her own belly.

They ate in silence, and while Red Doe was collecting the empty dishes, Heidr Tungl thanked them for the meal and praised them for the quality. Erik went around and shook everyone's hand.

They all laughed. Then Bull Moose looked hard into Heidr Tungl's eyes and said, "Tell me, Monongahela Woman, how did you kill this Great War Chief? Bull Moose needs to be ready in case you have any such plans for him." He gave her sort of a half-smile.

"Great Chief Bull Moose, I assure you that you have nothing to fear from me. That was a blood killing. He tortured and killed my mother and father in front of me—I had to take action against him. I would never violate your generosity by causing trouble in your village." She was completely taken aback that he knew anything about her past.

"Then you truly come in peace?"

"Yes, we are here to meet with the Norse and go back to Greenland with them. They are my husband's people."

He smiled. "What will you do? His world will not welcome you. Their shamans forbid them from bringing our people back to their lands as anything but slaves. The master of the great canoe, Bjarni, will probably refuse to take you. What then? Do you think you will make a home here? I expect not. Whenever one of our maidens gives birth to one of pale skin, we give it to the gods. Our people and their kind do not mix. I would have your children killed if you stay here. Did you know that when this great canoe leaves our shores, they will not be welcome back here ever again? If they return, we will kill every last one of them. You should plan to go with Salmon Eye and his band."

"Bull Moose, I have lived my life without fear. Yel...Tor, with me at his side, will ride the great canoe to the land of the Norse where we will make our life together. He will be a great chief among them, and I will give him many children. My spirit helper, Wolf—First Man, himself, has told me this." She paused for effect, then looked coldly into his eyes. "Great Chief, if you threaten a child of mine, I will see you dead." The promise in her face ran a chill down his spine. Bull Moose started to rise up, but he withered under her hard glare.

Blue Jay spoke up with a big smile and trepidation in his voice. "Heidr Tungl, do you think Erik has had enough food? Perhaps you should return to the Norse tent now."

"Yes, on both counts." She kept her eyes on Bull Moose, who looked like he did know what to do with himself.

"Go then," he finally said, "and rely on the Norse for your needs."

"I thank you for your hospitality, Great Chief. White Goose and Red Doe, your food was delicious, and I thank you for sharing. Come, Erik, we will go back to your father now." Heidr Tungl stood and walked to the entrance. Blue Jay followed to the Norse tent.

"I have never seen anyone quiet father like that!" The awe in his voice and on his face were unmistakable.

"I cannot let anyone threaten my children. I hope you understand."

"Oh, I understand. You were amazing! Do you think I could come with you?" Blue Jay blurted out.

"You mean to the Norse tent?"

"No. To the lands of the Norse. I want to be your slave. Your strength is more powerful than anything in my world!"

"I think you belong here. You will be the great chief one day. Everyone you know will depend on you." She was less than confident in her words. Blue Jay did not strike her as the type who would make a great leader.

"Me? I will never be chief of anything. Father thinks I am useless because I am happy all the time —even when he beats me. I must laugh it off because I am not strong enough to do anything else. It makes my heart hurt more than my body, so I use laughter to hide my shame. As a result, no one takes me seriously. So, I laugh my way from day to day."

"You are barely more than a child. You will

grow strong. Work hard on getting stronger, and you will be fine." She felt sorry for him.

When Heidr Tungl reentered the Norse tent, Tor was telling his tale of surviving the storms in the great Norse canoe his father had made.

Salmon Eye and his warriors had left the tent and were in one of the empty Micmac longhouses. Broken Bow stayed with Tor, wishing to learn what he could of the Norse.

When they returned, Tor took Erik into his arms and never stopped talking in the strange Norse tongue. Erik was soon sound asleep. Heidr Tungl took him to a pile of skins one of the Norsemen pointed for her to lie on. She was soon sleeping peacefully herself.

Tor spoke and answered questions well into the night. He helped the Norse devour half of a roasted moose. Bjarni apologized that their mead supply had run out, so they had to drink water or bitter tea. As Tor told of Heidr Tungl's life, they looked over at her in her peaceful repose with disbelief. "Surely such a beauty could never harm a man!"

"I pray to God that I am never tested against her...I have seen her fight, and she frightens me. Her love for me is the greatest gift I could ever ask of God."

"You will need to keep a close eye on her if you

intend not to share her among this lot." Bjarni waved his arm around the tent to the Norsemen, most of whom had their eyes glued on Heidr Tungl.

"In response, I will say this: Any man among you who chooses to lay a hand on her, I promise I will kill you—if you survive her wrath. Most likely you will not live long enough to enjoy her. So just stay away from her. She is a kind person and will befriend any, and all, of you. But if you cross that line, she will have no hesitation to kill you. Am I clear on this? Answer me, each of you." Tor left no room for doubt. He looked at each man until he nodded his head. It was near dawn before the talking was finished, and they all went to sleep.

Heidr Tungl and Erik went outside after the sun rose. Tor and all the Norse were snoring loudly when they left the tent. She gave Erik a piece of venison jerky to chew on as she started to stroll toward the beach. Red Doe came up to her and asked if she needed anything.

"I wish to apologize for my father's rude behavior last night," Red Doe started.

"Oh, he was just being chief. I took no offense. I am the one to apologize. I reacted too harshly. I am sorry. I guess I was too tired to be polite."

"I think you reacted appropriately. If some strange chief threatened my child, I would react like you did. My father, chief or not, needed to be put in his place! You did it completely. Three of the maids who coupled with the Norse over the past few summers, bore children. Those children were put out to sea on a board before their first meal. All three of the maids took their own lives afterward. We cannot afford to keep losing our young maids this way. There must be something better."

"Tor says he wants to teach the Norse to treat your people, and all the people they meet, with respect and honor. Perhaps he can make a lasting peace between our peoples so that everyone benefits. Maybe that is why the gods put him and me together." Heidr Tungl looked at Red Doe like she could suddenly see in the dark.

"That is a beautiful thought, Heidr Tungl, but I fear the hearts of men are dark and will not choose the path leading to peace. They enjoy their war far too much. Our people have no reason to hate and make war on the Haudenosaunee fish eaters to the west but have been in bitter war with them as long as our memory of them speaks. Even if your Tor can make peace between his people and ours, there is no way he will stop the hate between us and the Haudenosaunee. Sadly, men are men, and we have to live with the consequences." Red Doe looped her arm through Heidr Tungl's arm. "Now, would you and Erik like some clam stew and rice cakes?"

"I do not think Bull Moose will welcome me back in his lodge. This arrangement is difficult for me to get used to. In most of the villages I have been in, the women own the houses and welcome whoever they wish, the men own nothing."

"That was always our way, the elders have said. But men were the war chiefs and the war with the Haudenosaunee has gone on so long that the men have gradually taken over as a practical solution."

"I have to get used to it. Tor tells me that men own everything in his world."

"It is not so bad. Actually, we women just let men think they control everything. But Bull Moose knows when he crosses the line with White Goose. I think you will find Bull Moose much more cordial today." Red Doe gave Heidr Tungl a sly smile.

CHAPTER 13
LEAVING TURTLE ISLAND

Later that day, Bjarni announced to Tor that they had all their trees cut and would be leaving before the Equinox, which was eight days away. "What are your plans? Do you expect free transport to Greenland?"

"We have some trade goods that should more than cover our expenses," Tor replied evenly.

"You really mean to take the Skræling back to Greenland?"

"You are a free man in the employ of Thorkell Rolfcarlsson, is that correct?"

"What does that have to do with anything?" Bjarni snapped back.

"As an employee of my uncle, you are also an employee of mine. If you know Thorkell at all, you know I speak the truth. Whether you are my employee or not, I will demand that you refer to my wife with respect. You will not refer to her as Skræling. Nor will you refer to any of these people as such. They are people with nations and names. The people in this cove are Micmac, not Skræling. My wife is my wife, and you will treat her with due respect. Is that clear?" Tor raised his voice to emphasize his point.

"You are a fool. I am master of this ship and these men. Do not think you can order me around! You have no proof that you are related to Thorkell, so why should I even believe you? Besides that, I have been faithful to him longer than you have been alive. Do you really think he would side with you? I say the Skræling wench stays here, and that is final. You can come along if I am happy with your payment. Otherwise, you will not come either."

Tor realized he went too far. He would not be able to intimidate Bjarni with his family connection to Thorkell until it was confirmed. *Perhaps I can threaten him with annihilation,* Tor thought to himself. "You know that Bull Moose and his people are ready to throw you out of their lands, do you not?" Tor replied calmly.

"What do you mean? We are friends here. We trade generously with these creatures. They will never miss the few trees we take. They welcome us every summer." Bjarni's voice reflected the slightest waiver in confidence.

"That is not what I have been told. You and your men have worn out your welcome by bringing the same pieces of wool cloth and poor-quality glass beads every year. Then you cut their trees indiscriminately, leaving ugly scars on the hillsides that allow the dirt to wash away with the rain. They say the forest is crying where you have been cutting the past five summers. They are also tired of the way your men treat their women."

"Their women beg my men to service them. That is no concern here. They are like children," Bjarni confidently answered.

"Did you know that whenever one of their maidens gives birth to a child with Norse blood, they kill it? They say that the Norse are uncivilized, having no manners or respect for the 'real' people. They do not want Norse blood tainting their offspring. You are only alive because Bull Moose is a generous host. But you have used up his patience. This will be your last venture into this bay. I can convince him that you are no brother of mine and get his men to make sure you do not leave this bay alive. Or you can listen to me and make some changes right now that will get you invited back here." He could see the crack in Bjarni's indomitable wall.

"You lie. The head man is afraid of us. He knows our weapons are superior and his men stand no chance against us." Bjarni spoke with bravado, but a nervous twitch betrayed his confidence.

"Really? And how many warriors can you get into battle formation in say, one hand of time? By the time you have your men dressed for battle, your ship will be set afire so you will be trapped here. Then they can just fade into the forest and pick you off one at a time. In a week, you'll be starving while they sit around laughing at you. Do you want to test that? I can make that happen. Or you can learn. What will it be?" Tor came back more confident than Bjarni. Tor watched Bjarni wilt.

"You will not get out of this tent to warn the beggars." Bjarni tried to sound threatening.

"Do you think I had not thought of that? My wife waits in Bull Moose's longhouse right now. If I do not come out of this tent alive, the entire Micmac people will be down on you like a swarm of bees," Tor replied convincingly, knowing he now had the upper hand.

"I will not trade metal weapons with these people," Bjarni said quietly.

"Do you have iron pots and kettles?"

"Only enough for our own use. We only

brought wool and those goat hair and wool hats Thorkell's thralls make."

"Perhaps a promise to bring pots and wool blankets rather than just strips of cloth and hats would make a difference," Tor replied.

"All right, you can do the talking since you speak their gibberish."

"And my wife and son are welcome to sail with you to Iceland?"

"What have you to trade for your passage?"

"I have some exotic skins, bear claws, teeth, and a few other things you might find interesting."

"Any gold?" Bjarni's eyes began to light up.

"Don't go getting greedy," Tor chided. "I will get my things. Wait here and let us keep this trade private."

Bjarni gave Tor a weak smile and looked through half-lidded eyes. "You drive a hard trade —like Thorkell. Maybe you *are* related."

"People, all people, need to be treated like they matter, Bjarni. It is a simple idea, but one that we Norse have forgotten."

"You seem to have learned a lot for one so young." Bjarni tried to sound conciliatory.

"I have seen a lot, from many angles, in my short life. And I have had some fine people to learn from." Tor spoke with pride.

Heidr Tungl greeted Tor with a big hug when

he appeared in the longhouse of Bull Moose. Erik wrapped himself around Tor's leg. "We will all be going to Iceland." Tor was relaxed for the first time since they left Sun Town.

"I am just happy to see you alive!" Heidr Tungl squeezed tears from her eyes.

"I need to take the bulk of our trade goods to Bjarni's tent to pay our way to Iceland. You need to stay here to make sure he does not reconsider our bargain. I had to put him in his place. He did not like that. But he is a reasonable man, and I think I convinced him to show some manners."

"Sounds like my experience here. Are we meant to fight, either with our fists or our tongues, our whole lives?"

"If we are to try to make things right in our world, the answer is yes," he replied and squeezed her shoulder for reassurance.

In three days, the Norse logging crew was back in camp. The twenty-five logs were being assembled into a large raft to be towed behind the ship to Brattahlid in Greenland. The two oxen that had been brought to haul the logs from the forest harvesting location to the river where they could be floated down to the bay were to be slaughtered and a great feast provided for the Norsemen and Micmac the evening before the Norse set sail for Greenland. They also brought along four sheep for the special feast at the end of their stay. There was no mead to be had, but the enterprising Norsemen had fermented some elderberries and made some wine.

Most of the Micmac from the fish camps had returned to make sure they outnumbered the Norse by at least two to one just to ensure the uneasy peace was kept. Tor and Heidr Tungl drank only the willow tea that White Goose had prepared.

As predicted, some of the Norse got drunk, loud, and rowdy. The Norse did their best to imitate the Micmac dancers around the big bonfire. The Micmac dancers politely allowed the staggering Norsemen to bounce around among them. Erik joined some Micmac children dancing off to the side and enjoyed himself. Despite the best efforts of Bull Moose and his most trusted warriors, at least a few of the Micmac maidens managed to slip into the darkness with Norse suitors. There would be more babies to send to the gods in the early summer unless his shaman could come up with enough squawroot to take care of the wayward maidens. The moon was high in the sky when the wine ran out, and the Norsemen began to sift into their big tent to sleep off the effects of the feast. When the Norsemen were quiet Bull Moose and his warriors relaxed, and those not on guard duty went to their lodges. Tor, Heidr Tungl, and Erik were now guests in Bull Moose's lodge.

The next morning, the Norse loaded everything onto the ship and prepared to cast off. They left their campsite littered with broken cups, dishes, wooden spoons, knife handles, axe handles, pieces of cloth, worn-out skins, and anything else they did not deem necessary for the voyage. They left their latrine trench uncovered and foul.

Bull Moose summoned Tor and Bjarni to his lodge while the Norsemen were loading the ship. "I have brought Tor here to interpret what I have to say, Norse. He is trustworthy and honest. I know his words will speak what I must tell you. When you first came to this village, your trade seemed fair. The animal-hair cloth and hats were something our women were happy to have. We thought the forest could spare a few trees. But now, five summers have passed, and you keep coming back and taking more trees. The forest is crying, and the forest spirits are screaming at me to stop it." He paused to let that sink in.

"Then there is the matter of your men fornicating with our young maidens. The maidens do not see the future like the elders do. I have tried to tell you that your men must stop this rude behavior. But they continue. I have no choice but to forbid you from coming back to our shores. If you, or any of your kind, return to this bay, you will not live to return to your homelands. Am I understood?" Bull Moose finished, his arms folded across his chest and a serious look on his face.

"Bull Moose, we have traded with you in good faith. We can bring more valuable trade goods for you. We have artists that carve magnificent things in wood or walrus ivory. We can bring walrus hides for your use, and much..."

Bull Moose put up his hand for Bjarni to stop. "It is your lack of manners and disrespect for our ways that breaks your welcome. We have been patient, thinking that being around civilized people would improve your behavior. We were wrong. You are no longer welcome here. And from what our recent Haudenosaunee guests have reported, your kind have had the same effects in their lands. I cannot welcome you back to these shores. Be gone now before my warriors decide they have seen enough of you. This is what I have to say."

"This is a threat you may live to regret," Bjarni warned Bull Moose.

"It is a promise, Norse. Now, leave my presence. Again, Bull Moose has spoken." Bull Moose turned and walked away, his entourage following him.

"No Skræling fool will threaten me," Bjarni snarled to Tor as they walked toward the ship. "We will be back with three ships full of warriors and take what we wish from these animals."

"I will not accompany you on that fool's mission," Tor said coolly. "My gut tells me they will be ready for you. They know this land far better than you. They will have a deadly surprise behind every tree."

"We will see." Bjarni's mood was dark.

CHAPTER 14
LEIFSBUDIR

Tor and his family were relegated to the livestock hold in the bottom of the ship. Bjarni advised Tor to stay with Heidr Tungl at all times because he could not guarantee the behavior of all of his men. While Erik played with his Micmac friends, Tor and Heidr Tungl put down several layers of white cedar bows to cover the floor of the filthy livestock hold for comfort, and to absorb the smell of the old manure. It had been two moons since the animals had been in the hold, but the damp belly of the ship did not give up its foul odor easily.

When the ship weighed anchor, they used two men to each of the fourteen oars to pull the ship and heavy raft of logs into the open water. They had to row the ship past the islands in the bay before Bjarni could catch the southwest wind with the sail. The winds were light, and the swells were not difficult to slide through. The ropes that attached the raft to the ship stretched and creaked as the ship found its way into the open water of the sea. Their course took them across open water for a day. Bjarni steered the ship to the northeast until a large island came into sight on the left side of the ship. They stayed off the coast while they followed it to the east. The movements of the ship were jerkier than anything Tor remembered from sailing as a boy. He attributed that to the heavy raft of logs they were towing. But the jerky movements made his stomach unsettled. Erik and Bright Moon were both using a bucket to catch their vomit.

Finally, he said, "Come with me, we are breaking Bjarni's orders and going up on the deck. You both need to move around to fend off the seasickness."

Just standing helped alleviate Heidr Tungl's queasiness. Erik was another matter. But as soon as his face hit the open air, he felt better. When they emerged onto the deck, Bjarni yelled from his place at the steerboard for Tor to come to him —alone. "I told you to keep them below! My men do not need to see a woman on the deck. You know the presence of a woman on the deck of a ship is a bad omen. You need to get them back below."

"They are seasick, they need fresh air. Let them breathe a little, and we will disappear again," Tor answered.

"Do not push me, Tor. I am master of this ship. There can only be one. What I say goes. Your woman's weak stomach is not my concern, getting this ship and raft to Brattahlid is. Now get your people below." Bjarni looked hard into Tor's eyes.

"Of course, you are the master. I just wanted them to get over the seasickness, but you are right, women do not belong on the sailing deck. My apologies." Tor nodded as he turned to get Heidr Tungl and Erik back below the top deck. They both felt better already.

"The shipmaster is the chief aboard a sailing ship, wife. His word is the way it is. I cannot argue that point. We will just have to get used to being down here. In a few days, we will be stopping at *Leifsbudir* where we can get our feet on the ground and walk around, breathe fresh air, and so on. From there, with a favorable wind, it will be just a few days to Brattahlid. We will be there for a couple days before we depart for Borg in Iceland. Winter will be upon us by the time we reach there, I think. Our buffalo robes will keep us warm. I am glad we did not trade them away." He tried to sound optimistic.

"Why are we unwelcome up there?" She pointed to the opening to the top deck.

"The old sailors always said that a woman on a ship would bring bad luck. Storms and evil serpents would devour ships that carried women. Funny, at the same time, there are stories of great Shieldmaidens who sailed among the great raiders. A few even owned their own ships," he said as he shook his head, smiling.

"Shieldmaidens?" Heidr Tungl asked.

"A few, very few, women have taken up the warrior mantle among the Norse. Those women, who go into battle and fight alongside men, are known as Shieldmaidens."

"So, I am a Shieldmaiden, since I fought alongside you?"

"I had not thought of that, but yes, I suppose so." He smiled into her face.

She nodded and buried her face in his chest.

"Papa. Smell...bad!" Erik tugged on Tor's tan hunting shirt as he looked up and made a sour face.

"Yes, my son, it does smell bad down here—almost as bad as your pants do sometimes. Soon we will be on land again and can go out running and breathing fresh air." Tor bent down and picked up the small boy. "You are getting so big!" *This year has passed so quickly!* he thought as he recalled the child's birth in Sun Town, a year past. *I pray I am doing the right thing, tearing them from their world and bringing them to mine.*

BJARNI SKILLFULLY STEERED the heavy ship between two encroaching land masses. The weather had been favorable for two days as they approached the narrow channel between Markland on their port side and Vinland on their steerboard side. It had become obvious that more lands lay to the west since Leif Erikson had named these places nearly thirty years earlier, but they stayed with the name of Vinland for everything south and west of Markland. Troubles with the Skræling inhabitants of Markland and much of Vinland made them search farther for the timber needed for the building of the settlements of Greenland and repairing ships.

Five years earlier, Thorkell Rolfcarlson had discovered the Micmac in the bay they had just vacated. Thorkell made peace with the Micmac, and they had carried out the trade for timber ever since. But now, Bjarni's lack of discipline among his men had led to the loss of the Micmac land as a friendly source to quench Greenland's thirst for lumber.

Leif Erikson's outpost, Leifsbudir, remained the only permanent Norse outpost in Vinland. There they would be able to safely put ashore, check the ship over, and make repairs before setting out across the open water to Greenland. For many years, the course had been to follow the Markland coast to Helluland, then turn east and sail to the Western Settlements and on south from there to Eriksfjord and Brattahlid. A new town called Gardar was now being built on Einarsonsfjord just east of Brattahlid. Over the years, a route was plotted to take a southwest course from Eriksfjord across open water to Leifsbudir. This course would save around four sailing days. The winds pushing through the narrow strait between Markland and Vinland increased their speed markedly. Well before darkness set in, Tor heard the men shouting orders to lower the sail and prepare to land as they slipped into the small bay where Leifsbudir was located.

———

HEIDR TUNGL and Erik joyfully ran the grassy ridges around the outpost, glad to be free of the confines of the smelly hold of the ship. The grass had withered from its summer growth and turned the color of Erik's hair. Tor helped the men pull the ship and the raft of logs to the shore. After just a few days at sea, some of the ropes were frayed and needed to be replaced.

Just before landing, they ran onto a herd of seals that were easy prey. They took enough to have a great feast and some to take for the journey from there to Brattahlid. Before she could object, Bright Moon was stirring fresh rice, some sort of bog roots, and seal meat in large iron kettles. She had never seen anything like those big kettles. Erik did what he could to sort the rice grain from the wet plants men had cut and brought into the hall.

There was little more than a large hall where they would sleep, cook, and eat. There was also a small forge where iron could be worked into useful items, a sawmill, and tubs for rendering fat. No permanent residents lived there, but crews would spend the summers there making ship repairs and doing whatever else the shipmasters ordered. Due to increased problems with the Skræling, they were kept busy making weapons like arrow and spear points and shields. The summer residents raised a few sheep, which they transported back to Greenland at summer's end. When Bjarni guided Thorkell's ship up to the wooden dock, the summer crew had left a few days prior.

The ship was at the dock for two days while repairs to riggings were made and some of the ropes on the log raft were replaced.

During the short stay at Leifsbudir, a Norseman named Egill Hallundsson made the mistake of putting his hand on Heidr Tungl's bottom while her attention was focused on the big pot of seal meat stew. Tor was at the ship working on the rigging at the time. Her elbow drove into Egill's nose so hard he was knocked unconscious. When he woke up moments later, his mouth was full of blood, his nose misshapen, blood all over his face and down his tunic. Heidr Tungl stood over him with the paddle she used to stir the stew, ready to finish the job, if he was inclined to advance his desires further. Several of the men were watching to see how she would react when one of them got up the courage to touch her. Two came over and helped him to his feet and escorted him outside where he could clean up. One looked her in the eye and nodded approvingly.

The men working on the ship were finished and just coming up to the hall when Egill was being helped to a water barrel. Bjarni snarled, "Who have you been fisting with now, Egill?" A man named Rolf was helping him and started laughing. "What would be so funny?" Bjarni demanded. Tor had his suspicions.

"He might be good with an axe, Master Bjarni, but not worth a wit in a fight with a woman." Rolf laughed as he spoke.

"Fight?"

"Not a fight, really. He laid a hand on her bottom, and she rearranged his nose before he knew what happened. Knocked him out cold, she did. Laid him out like a fallen tree. He could not look more pathetic. Hehe."

"Get him cleaned up and reset his nose. This better not happen again!" Bjarni glared at Tor.

"I will go check on her." Tor stepped into the hall.

"Egill tried to put his hands on you? Are you all right?"

"Yes, I am fine, how is he?"

"His nose is spread across his face, but he will live. His pride is probably in worse shape than his nose," Tor answered her.

"What happened?" Tor pressed.

"I was stirring the stew when suddenly there was a hand on my bottom. I give him credit for sneaking up on me. I am getting careless. I could tell where his face would be by the way his hand was on my bottom. I jerked my elbow into his face, and he went down. That was about all that happened." She turned to stir the stew again.

"Did Erik see it? How did he react?" Tor asked

as he watched Erik concentrate on separating rice seed from the chaff.

"He was doing what he is now. I was concerned about what Egill and the others might do, I had my back to Erik. But he came over to me and said something about the man being hurt. I told him the man's friends will make him better. He went back to his job after I hugged him. He did not seem to even notice the blood soaking into the dirt floor." She did not look up from the stew pot.

Tor looked around, and every eye in the hall was watching him and Heidr Tungl. No one was talking or even moving. Tor looked at each man, who then turned away and took up conversations with each other. Word quickly spread that the Skræling woman could take care of herself.

The next morning was partly cloudy, and thick frost covered every outdoor surface. The distant forest almost looked like it was covered in new snow. As they were loading the ship, Bjarni's men stopped and watched as Heidr Tungl gracefully traipsed up and down the ladder to the animal hold cleaning and replacing the cedar bows with fresh cut dwarf spruce used to cover the floor. They were amused that she carried herself so well with her pregnant belly protruding. Their looks and leers of disdain had been replaced by a new look of respect.

WHEN THE SUN was less than a hand above the horizon, they caught the outgoing tide and slid into the open ocean. Fog was drifting across the water, so lookouts were posted at the bow to watch for rocks until they made their way into the open ocean. Ice was of little concern in that season. Their course would take them north-northeast for three days, when they would see the coast of Greenland. Bjarni was met with cheers of approval when the sheet filled, and they sailed for civilization. A westerly breeze pushed them for two days.

The stars at night had been accompanied by green and purple curtains of The Lights. Tor brought Heidr Tungl and a sleepy Erik up to watch the lights wavering in the northern sky. "I have never seen them this close. It seems they will come right down and touch us. Do their spirits bring evil or good?" She squeezed a little tighter to him, as if he could protect her from such powerful spirits.

"They just are. I do not think they are alive or spirits. Just something about how the light from the moon or stars shines up there. Perhaps there is a series of holes in the ice in the north, and great green and red lights from deep in the earth shine through those holes. I know not." Tor looked at the lights deep in the memory of his father's story of the lights that led him to the gates of Valhalla in his dream out on the northern ice many years past.

The third morning they woke up to a low, gray sky and cold drizzle. The wind barely fluttered the wool sail and progress was slow. Gradually the sun poked a few holes in the overcast sky and a south wind picked up. By evening the sky was mostly clear, the white tops of Greenland's snow-covered hills visible.

CHAPTER 15

HRYN REGINNSWIFE

The next day when they entered Eriksfjord, Bjarni summoned Tor to the steerboard. "You can bring your wench up on the deck if you like. We have passed the dangerous part of our journey. She should get a look at civilization before it smacks her in the face."

"Your kindness is touching, Master." Tor smiled at Bjarni.

The ship was still under sail as they made their way up the fjord. Heidr Tungl saw mostly reeds and water channels at first. Small willow and birch trees lined the banks of the fjord in many places, but soon the expanses between the waterways gave way to grassy pastures. An occasional flock of sheep, accompanied by a dog and a boy, were seen gleaning the last of the green grass from the pastures. On a small island, she saw the first Norse farm occupied by a family. It was one main building with two small outbuildings.

The main house was shaped like a squat long-house with sod walls and a thickly grassed roof. Smoke rose from a stone chimney near one end of the hall. A small stone fence made a square shape past one end of the hall. A few sheep, goats, and two brown cows were in the rock fence enclosure.

Tor had to explain what the animals were and what they were used for. "I have so much to learn before I fit in this world," she said softly to him. She noted smoke rising from a tiny hole in one of the outbuildings. Tor explained that the Norse cure their meat by smoking it in the little house. The main house had a door that led to a path leading to a small landing. There was a strange, odd-shaped canoe tied up to a small rock dock there. The canoe was made of wooden planks somehow fastened together. Tor explained to her the construction of small fishing boats. She nodded her head but did not understand. Erik pointed to a large dog that chased a small child around the yard while a woman picked something out of a small garden. The woman wore clothing that looked completely foreign to her. "So much to learn," Heidr Tungl said to nobody.

As the ship eased past the small farm, Heidr Tungl noted a door opening from the small pasture to the end of the house. "Why such a big door?"

Tor explained that many families have animal stalls in part of their lodges to protect the animals from the harsh winters and to help warm the house during those cold months. She shook her head in disbelief.

As they sailed farther up the fjord, more farms, halls, and people began to appear. Heidr Tungl noted a few people were moving along a path in the direction they were moving. Some were pointing toward Tor and her. *How do they make slaves of those big animals?* she asked herself.

Eventually, they came to a gathering of buildings strung along the edge of the fjord. On a rise was the prominent hall that Erik the Red had built and was now occupied by Leif Eriksson and his family. Bjarni ordered the sail lowered, and oars were placed in the water. A group of crude rock docks reached into the water. With Bjarni using the steerboard and the men with oars, they maneuvered the boat alongside a dock, and a couple of sailors jumped onto the dock and tied the ship to posts set in the ground. Using the ropes attached, they steered the log raft up along the shore next to the dock. Then they tied the raft to posts that were embedded in the bank for that purpose.

A throng of people had gathered and were talking among themselves. Some pointed to Tor, Heidr Tungl, and little Erik and scoffed at their animal skin clothes. Others shouted insults at Tor for his Skræling mistress. He ignored them and went about helping unload what was staying in Brattahlid.

Finally, Bjarni stepped in front of the noisy crowd, waved his arms over his head, and shouted for them to quiet down so he could talk. After they settled down, he explained, "Tor Eriksson had been lost at sea and washed ashore among the Skræling. He survived harrowing trials, eventually taking the woman for his wife. They obviously have a child, and she is in the family way now." They drew in a collective sigh at these words. Tension filled the gathering. "Tor Eriksson and his family will be reuniting with his uncle in Iceland." The gathering seemed to relax a bit.

"So long as the Skræling will not be a part of our lives, we could allow them to spend a night or two in Brattahlid. The Skræling are lazy, good-for-nothing thieves! Keep a close eye on them!" someone yelled out.

"They will seek the priest to convert the

woman to Christianity and baptize the boy," Bjarni told them, resulting in many voicing their objections.

"Looks a bit late for Christianity to set in, there are already two bastards in the pot. I'd say that stew is already cooked!" shouted someone from the rear of the crowd.

Tor stepped up and stood next to Bjarni. "I am Tor Eriksson, of Ulfrstadt, Norway. It is understandable that you have misgivings about people who are different from you."

"The Skræling are not people!" A voice rang out from somewhere in the crowd. "These Skræling cannot be people. Father Harald teaches this!"

"There are many people in the world who the priests know nothing about. I have met some of those people. I assure you, they are real, and they are people. Some of the people I met in my journey thought I must be a god because there were no people outside their world. Others thought I was a filthy foreigner up to no good. Of course, they were wrong, and it is wrong to think the unknown people we run into are Skræling. I have seen one of their cities that is bigger than any in our world. It is time we recognize them as the people they are. My wife and I will move on to Iceland in the next few days, but I ask you to look at our neighbors across the water as people, not creatures," Tor pleaded.

"You are welcome in my hall, Tor Eriksson." Hryn Reginnswife spoke up. "My man is off on a voyage to Norway and will not return until next summer. I could use the help for a few days."

"We wish to burden no one," Tor replied.

"It is no burden. You will earn your keep," Hryn replied. "Besides, your woman and child need a bed to sleep in—I can see to that. Go make their bedding, Cairenn."

"Delighted to, mistress Hryn." A young woman with long, orange-colored hair in a drab cloth dress nodded and scurried off toward the unorganized group of buildings up the slope from the docks.

"It is settled then, get your belongings and follow me," Hryn said to Tor. The rest of the crowd backed away murmuring among themselves.

"Reginn Englarsson will not be happy when he gets wind of this! You best sleep with an axe in your hand! Reginn's household is forfeit!" shouts echoed from the dispersing crowd that had gathered at the dock.

"Pay them no mind." Hryn looked to Heidr Tungl as she spoke. "God will punish those with small minds in the afterlife for their hatred and unchristian ways. God's children are to be charitable."

Laden with heavy packs, Tor and Heidr Tungl followed Hryn to her modest hall in an uneven row of similar looking buildings. Erik skipped along between his parents, happy to be out of the dreary ship's belly. Outwardly the houses looked much like mounds of dirt covered with grass with wooden frames and doors in the south walls. Heidr Tungl was awed by the thick door hung on hinges. She had never seen anything like that before. *They work magic here!* she thought. She hesitantly followed the others through the opening.

Inside, the floor was covered with flat rocks fitted close together. They were worn smooth from foot traffic. The walls were also rocks fitted together up to about chest high, then a wood frame with sod blocks between the posts rose to just over head high. A thick wood beam topped the wall and heavy wood beams and rafters framed the roof. Woven grass and reeds lay on top of wooden slats that tied the rafters together. Over the reed mats was a thick layer of sod that was visible from outside the house. One end of the rooms was dominated by a large rock fireplace. Various iron pots and cookware sat atop the rock hearth. A heavy iron, arched hook was hinged on one side of the fireplace. A pot hung on the hook that could be swung over the hot coals for heating the contents, which currently had an odd smelling stew bubbling in it. Some cakes like none Heidr Tungl had ever seen were in small square pots sitting on a flat iron plate in one part of the fireplace. The smoke rose through a rock tunnel that rose from the top of the fireplace and up through the roof. Chunks of driftwood lay in a box by the fireplace to be added to the fire as needed.

In the center of the room was a raised platform of rocks with two large flat rocks on top of it. Wooden benches were positioned on either side of the rock platform and large metal bowls with metal spoons were set in an orderly fashion around the table. At the other end of the house was a wood framed wall covered with woven reed mats. A door opening with a heavy cloth door hanging led to a small room. On the big room side of the wall, three beds were set up. Two were large enough for two people to share and the smaller one would hold one adult. One of the larger beds had a headboard that was carved intricately with filigree and dragon heads.

"The boy will sleep in the small bed, and Cairenn will sleep in the big bed with me while you are here. We have three beds because my husband likes to share his house with sailors who do not live in Greenland. They pay him for room and board. Cairenn usually sleeps in the small bed, but sometimes must sleep on the floor when Reginn brings too many to fit in one bed. She has come of age now and that may cause problems in the future with some of our guests."

Hryn talked nonchalantly. Heidr Tungl had to pay very close attention to understand the Norse tongue. And Cairenn had an odd way of saying the Norse words.

"There is some space in the back room for the things you won't be needing in here," she said to Tor.

He took their packs through the door hanging into the small room.

"Sit down." Hryn indicated for Heidr Tungl to sit at the table. "You must be tired from all your days of traveling. Cairenn, bring some tea and those honey biscuits for little Erik." She patted Erik on the head. He had lost that baby eider duck look as his hair grew longer. It had bleached almost white during the long sunny days of the summer while riding in the canoes. "He will be a handsome one, like his father."

"I was a young sprout, just a few years older than your boy when my father brought us here from Iceland. The voyage across the sea frightened me to death. Before that, we had moved from Norway, but I have no memory of that voyage. I spent much of the time with my head in a wooden bucket retching up everything I ate. And the men would not allow us on the deck because children and women on deck would bring bad luck. We stayed the whole time on the second deck just above the smelly animals. That boat ride could not end soon enough for me. And when we got here, there was little to behold. Erik the Red's great hall stood on the hill of course. It is Leif's now. And his mother's little church. Oh, there were a few other buildings in all of Greenland then, mostly right around here. We slept in tents, and the men worked all day cutting rocks, sod blocks, and wood framing for the houses. Many people came at that time, and there was much activity. My brothers and I spent most of those first summers tending sheep out in the pastures. I was homesick for my friends back in Iceland, but soon learned to love it here. I talk too much, tell me about you." Hryn barely took a breath from talking so fast.

"I have much to learn. It is all too much for me, right now," Heidr Tungl answered.

"Yes, I suppose so," Hryn said slowly.

"If you ladies are all right here, I will go back to the ship and help Bjarni get her ready to sail again. There are many small repairs to be made before we set out for Iceland," Tor interrupted.

Erik was quick about getting himself off the

bench and next to Tor. "You are too small, my son. The work is too dangerous, and I cannot watch you all the time. I will be back soon."

Erik was bruised by his father's rejection, but he knew he would have to stay with his mother in the dark house. At least the air did not smell awful.

Before long, Erik was bored enough to lie down on the bed and fell asleep.

"Tell me what snares you used to trap such a fine man?" Hryn asked pointedly.

"Snares?" Heidr Tungl asked. "I do not know about snares for men. I had never been interested in any man. My sister fell in love with an enemy who turned out not to be an enemy. They are happily married in the lands where I was born. But me, I never wanted anything to do with men except to fight one of them. He was the only man I ever thought about. After I destroyed him, I was lost. I saw no future. Then Yellow Hair, Tor, came down the river, and my whole world changed. I know not whether it was the Christian God, the gods of my world, or the gods of Cahokia who brought us together. But once we saw one another, we both knew where we belonged. Much has happened since that day at the canoe landing at Monongahela Village, but our love for each other is undiminished. Am I saying the right words?"

"Your story sounds like one that legends are

made from. Who was this man you killed?" Hryn asked cautiously.

"An evil war chief. Not worth talking about, really. He killed my mother and father, and my sister and I paid him back." Heidr Tungl looked at nothing as she spoke. "Tor lost his whole family in those storms. I want him to reclaim his life."

"Even though it means losing yours?"

"Yes, it means that much. After the war chief killed my parents, Wolf came to me and told me what I must do. After I did that, he promised me nothing. When Tor came into my life, Wolf encouraged me to go with him across the big water. He said that once I cross the big water, he can no longer protect me, that Tor's people will hate me and hurt me. I promised I will remain strong—my love for Tor overshadows all else. Wolf also said that I will give Tor many children. They will grow up as Tor's children, be of his people. Now, after nearly two sun cycles of travel, we are close to Tor's people, and Wolf's words are coming true, as always." Heidr Tungl talked with honesty in her voice.

"Remarkable," Hryn said softly. "And who is Wolf? In my world, wolves are vicious, evil beasts who kill humans just for fun."

"Ugh!" Heidr Tungl snapped. "Wolf is First Man! He made the rest of us. He opened the way.

We would not exist without him. Tor has warned me that the Christian world is blind to everyone but themselves. They need to open hearts and minds and listen to other peoples' truths. Your people would see me as a heathen, locked in a cage to wither and die. But I am no heathen. I love and laugh just like you. I bleed every moon when I am not pregnant. I feel warmth for you and your people. I will learn the Christian world and be part of it. And I will always hold on to what I have always known. Wolf, Eagle Man, Raven, Coyote, Woodpecker, Turtle, Horned Serpent, and Water Panther are all just as real as any other god. All the peoples have their own way of seeing the gods. And they are all under the Great Creator Spirit. To crush someone else's beliefs because you think yours are better is evil. Do I make sense to you?"

"You shake me to the core, woman. I think it best that we no longer talk about this subject. I want to care about you, to be your friend, but if you are to renounce my god, then we cannot be friends," Hryn replied remorsefully.

"I do not renounce your god, Hryn, I welcome him. I want to love him. But to ask me to renounce what I have been taught my whole life is also not acceptable." Heidr Tungl tried to sound conciliatory.

Hryn looked sadly at Heidr Tungl. "Poor child,

you have not had the teaching yet. I will not judge you, but I will tell you that the Christian God says in his own words that he is the only true God, and there will be no gods before him. Now, let us talk no more of this. Tell me about your dress, what animal is it made from? Did you make it yourself?"

"All right, to be friends, we will look past our different beliefs, I can do that. My dress is made from the hide of a white-tailed deer. A very common animal in my world. It is smaller than your, uh, cow, but looks a little like one. I have seen caribou skins and antlers here, deer are about their size, but the antlers are much different. I have seen some clothes made from your sheep skins. Until we made it to the Norse camp in the land of the Micmac, I had never seen a sheep. The cloth you make from their hair interests me a great deal." Heidr Tungl spoke with enthusiasm in her voice as she studied Hryn's dress.

"We separate the wool fibers with these combs, spindles, and whorls to make thread from it. The sheep grow long, thick hair over the winter, and we sheer it off in the early summer. Our Greenland wool is prized in Norway. It is because the grass here is so rich that the wool is superior to anywhere else. Depending on the cloth we want to make, we can leave the thread heavy and coarse, or separate it until it is thin and fine. For heavy winter clothes and blankets we make coarse thread, and for undergarments and summer clothes, we make fine thread. The threads are then woven on a loom." She pointed to her loom against the side wall of the big room. "By using different colored thread, we can make different colored cloth, or patterns in the cloth.

"I have made a tapestry of the things that have happened in our lives since Reginn Englarsson and I were married." She pointed to the wall to one side of the table where a cloth hung that showed two people standing together and a man holding out his hands toward the couple. Another part showed men on a sailing ship. Three others showed a couple putting a small child in what looked like a grave. Much of the cloth was blank. "We have only been married eight years. Much of our story is yet to be told. We can also use special needles to knit the threads together to make many things, such as hats, scarfs, or mittens."

"Some of our people make story belts with beads that tell a village history, a family history, or some important event. When last I saw her, my sister was making a story belt telling our story from our mother being killed to me destroying that evil war chief." Heidr Tungl spoke like she was telling how to put a bead on a string.

"This 'war chief,' did he have a name?"

"Yes, but when a person dies, especially in a violent way, we never speak his name aloud. That could call his evil spirit, and I do not want that to happen. He has visited me in dreams many times, and those are not good dreams," Heidr Tungl answered.

CHAPTER 16

HEIDI

Hryn could not understand how the young woman could talk so calmly about killing a man. "I could never kill a man. Do you mind if I call you Heidi? It would be an easier way to say *Heidr Tungl*. How can you talk so calmly about it? Is it not forbidden to kill people in your country? What does your religion say about killing other people?"

Cairenn was busy playing with Erik and preparing the evening meal, but she stopped and looked at Heidr Tungl to see her reaction to Hryn's question.

"If you wish to name me Heidi, I have no objection, it has a good sound, I like it. Understand that I would never kill anyone who was not trying to kill me or someone I love. There are evil people,

people out of balance with the spiral. They must be stopped before the world gets out of balance and is destroyed. Only when the world is in balance can there be harmony and peace. If I am called upon to help bring harmony back to the world, then that is what I must do. Of course, taking another life for no reason is forbidden among my people. People who are guilty of murder are put to death themselves, if they are caught," Heidr Tungl answered nonchalantly.

"May I ask Heidi a question, Mistress Hryn?" Cairenn asked, looking at her feet. Her Norse tongue was as broken as Heidi's and had an odd accent that made it more difficult to keep up with.

"Do you mind?" Hryn looked at Heidi.

"Of course not. I just hope I can understand and answer correctly. My ears and tongue have not gotten used to the Norse yet."

Nervously, Cairenn talked very slowly, but quietly so that Heidi had to ask her to repeat the question, which made Cairenn more nervous. "What men have you killed? How did you over-power them?"

"Cairenn! That is not a proper question for a young woman to ask a guest in this house!" Hryn raised her voice. "Apologize and hold your tongue! Or I shall have to beat you!"

"Hryn, it is all right. Perfectly good questions.

Do you mind if I answer the girl?" Heidi spoke quickly.

"I do not think you should answer in front of the child." Hryn looked nervously from Heidi to Cairenn to Erik, who had woken and was busy playing with a loom weight, not paying heed to the women anyway. "Answer if you please, but do not feel obligated."

"Cairenn, after my mother was murdered, I spent nine sun cycles, um, years preparing to fight the man who did it. He was a huge man, powerful and evil. He had killed many men, women, and children by the time I confronted him. I had to learn to beat the man who was said to be the greatest warrior our world had ever known. A wise friend told me that I would never be stronger or faster than my enemy, but I could be smarter and quicker. He told me to learn to catch bugs, birds, and small animals using just my hands without being bitten. After I mastered the small animals, I moved up to snakes and big birds.

"Finally, I was ready. My sister and I lured the evil man into a forest. We fought with war clubs —kind of like your axes. I thought I would die, but, after a time, was able to injure him over and over until he was weakened. Once he was down, I wanted him to feel pain, like my mother and father felt. My sister helped with that part, as was her right. The point is, I learned to deal with evil. Unfortunately, I have learned that evil did not stop with that one evil man. I have had to defend myself, or Tor, more than a few times since then. Did I answer your question?" Heidi had to get down on her knees to look up into Cairenn's eyes.

"Yes." Cairenn turned back to the big pot of stew.

Hryn looked sadly at Heidi. "Heidi, God, through his son, The Christ, tells us to turn the other cheek, and to love our enemy, not smite him. You will learn to deal differently with evil men from the priest at Myrar Borg. He is a fine teacher, I am told."

"I have much to learn, and I hope the Christian God can protect my family from evil people, but I will do as I must to protect them." Heidi looked firmly into Hryn's eyes. Hryn looked back, but soon turned away. Heidi's determination was over-powering.

A long silence followed that was interrupted by the door opening. Tor came in with a worn out look on his face. Erik was up and hugging Tor's leg before his eyes adjusted to the candlelight in the room. Tor picked up Erik and held him high exclaiming, "See, I came back! And you are just fine." Erik giggled, kicking feet and flailing arms while Tor held him in the air, nearly touching the low ceiling.

"I have a new name!" Heidi smiled as she got up and walked toward Tor and Erik. "Hryn thinks I should be called 'Heidi,' and I like the sound of it. What do you think?"

"Heidi is a good name. I admit it is easier to say," Tor answered. "Thank you for the new name, Hryn. You are already a good friend. What work do you have that I can do for you?" Tor asked Hryn.

"It can wait until tomorrow. It is getting late. Let us enjoy the good lamb and cabbage stew Cairenn has prepared for us," Hryn replied as she motioned them to the table. Cairenn took the bowls and filled them one at a time and set them in front of everyone. She put loaves of the strange looking cakes on a plate and set it in the middle of the table. Next, she poured each person a cup of willow leaf tea flavored with honey. Then, she poured Erik a small wooden cup of cow's milk. She set a small bowl with a whitish looking paste next to the loaves and placed a wide knife next to it. Finally, she set out a plate with a round disk of a whitish substance and took a knife and sliced pieces of it. When everyone had their food in front of them, she made a dish for herself and sat at the table next to Hryn.

Hryn took Cairenn's hand and Heidi's hand,

indicating that they all hold hands. Next, she bowed her head and said a prayer of thanks for their food to the Christian God. In her prayer, she asked God to forgive Heidi of her sins and teach her the "Way." "You see, Heidi, all good things come from God, and it is incumbent upon us to thank him for all we have, even the small things."

"Of course, you are right, Hryn." Heidi smiled, hiding her real reaction to Hryn's insinuation that Heidi was a savage. As she sampled the stew, questions arose in her mind about the ingredients. She learned she would need to get used to cabbage as it was a mainstay in the Norse diet. The cakes, she learned, were made from the self-sown wheat the Norse harvested. And the white paste was butter churned from cow milk, while the cheese was made both from cow and goat milk. *So much to learn!* rattled in her brain.

Tor gave an update on the ship repairs. He said they would be ready to sail in three days. "Bjarni wants to get to Iceland before any winter storms decide to make an appearance. Clouds appear to be gathering in the north this evening. We may have rain by morning."

"My fall garden could use a little rain," Hryn added.

By sunrise, a dense fog enshrouded the town, and a cold mist was making everything wet. Tor went to work repairing a sheep stall in Hryn's back room while Heidi accompanied Cairenn down to the trader booths to see what she could get for a couple of cabbage heads and some mint from Hryn's garden. Erik stayed with Tor, and Hryn worked at her loom.

At the trader booths, as soon as people noticed Heidi dressed in an oiled deerskin jacket and decorated moccasins, they started in with derogatory remarks. "Here comes that Skræling thief, hide your wares!", "There is no space here for your kind!", "Go back and steal Hryn's things, we have no use for you here!" and so on. Cairenn spoke up. "She is no thief!"

"Says the Irish slave. No better than a thief, yourself, lassie!" someone yelled, followed by loud laughter.

"I think Hryn Reginnswife will not be happy to learn that ye good Christians treated her employee and guest with such disdain," Cairenn snapped back.

A young Norseman in a fine leather tunic and sporting an oiled dark beard stepped forward and grabbed Cairenn's arm and said, "Let's you and me slip to the back room of Skallar's shop and see if you talk about *disdain* when we're through!" Several men laughed. Heidi stepped in and drove her foot into the inside of the young man's forearm so fast and hard, he did not know what hit him. He held his arm and looked around for his assailant.

A friend stepped forward with a hand on his sword hilt. A loud voice came from off to the side. It was Egill, with his bruised face and swollen nose. His sword was drawn. "Back off, Svienn! You are no match for this woman. And Thorimm, take your wounded arm and go home. These women were minding their own business. Now, the rest of you, treat these two with respect. They will trade fairly. Any more trouble, and I will see to it that Bjarni's crew shuts down the lot of you. Understand?" A few nodded, the rest turned and went about their own business.

"Thank you, Egill, I did not know how that was going to go, but I could not let that man harm Cairenn," Heidi said sincerely.

"Happy to be of service, uh, I forgot your proper name." Egill looked around, embarrassed.

"I have a new, easier name. It is 'Heidi.' I expect you know Cairenn?" Heidi smiled.

"Have not made her acquaintance, actually." Egill smiled, looking at Cairenn, who was looking at the ground as close to her feet as she could look, cheeks flushed.

"Her name is Cairenn. She is the house servant of Hryn Reginnswife. We are here to trade for some food," Heidi replied, not knowing how to take

Egill's friendliness. After all, five days past, she had broken his nose and given him the ugly bruising about his eyes and cheeks.

"We set sail in two days, but I wonder if Hryn Reginnswife would allow me to court the young Cairenn?" Egill asked Heidi while he held his gaze on Cairenn. Egill's voice had a nasal twang to it.

"I expect you should ask Hryn that question," Heidi replied and looked for a reaction from Cairenn.

"Can I follow you back to her hall?"

"First, we must do our trading before we can return to the hall," Heidi answered, still not sure what Cairenn thought.

"Perhaps I should escort you—to make sure there is no more trouble," he said coyly.

"Do you object?" Heidi asked Cairenn, who kept her eyes glued to the ground and barely nodded her head. Egill smiled so wide; Heidi could see the pain in his bruised face.

They traded the cabbages for a large sack of rice and the mint for some sage and rosemary. Egill volunteered to carry the heavy sack back to Hryn's hall. They got looks in the trader booths, but no more hateful remarks.

"Hryn, this man, Egill Hallundsson, helped us in the trader booths and offered to carry this sack of rice that I traded the cabbage for," Cairenn said almost apologetically when they walked in the door of Hryn's hall.

"And what trouble was there at the trader booths that you needed help?" Hryn looked from Cairenn to Heidi to Egill.

"There was no trouble, lady Hryn. I saw these women struggling with the heavy sack of rice and offered to carry it for them," Egill offered.

"I asked Cairenn, but since you offered, I will tell you that you told a lie. And I do not hold to lying under my roof. Now, who wants to speak the truth?" Hryn demanded, looking from Cairenn to Heidi.

Cairenn started to speak, but Heidi cut her off before any word escaped her mouth. "A man named Thorimm at Skallar's shop grabbed Cairenn by the arm. If I understood correctly, he planned to take to the back of a booth and force himself upon her. I stepped in and kicked his arm and made him lose his grip on her arm. Some of the young men did not think I should have done that. Egill, here, stepped in, and the men backed away. There was no trouble after that. Egill has a question for you."

"You mean Thorimm Hrolfgersson? You realize he is of an important family in Brattahlid? He could make trouble for you, for me. Why did you hurt him? You might have gotten the same result by talking to him," Hryn scolded.

"I saw the intent in his eyes, there was no talking to him. Men like that need to be taught lessons. I gave him a small one." Heidi held her head high, maintaining eye contact with Hryn.

"You always fight first, don't you? God be with you, woman." Hryn shook her head.

"She is right, Mistress Hryn. He was going to hurt me. He already hurt my arm." She showed Hryn the bruise already visible on her arm.

"I know Thorimm, he expects all women to worship him. Your servant would have been damaged if Heidi had not stepped in. She is a brave one," Egill offered.

"You know this man?" Hryn asked Heidi.

"I got forward with her in Leifsbudir, Hryn. She put me in my place." Egill pointed to his face.

Just then, Tor and Erik came in from the back of the hall. Tor saw everyone standing like they were about to pitch into battle. "What is this all about? Egill, what are you doing here?" He stood in front of Egill. Erik ran and clung to Heidi.

"I helped these women at the trader booths and carried the rice back here for them. I was hoping to ask Hryn for permission to court Cairenn, but that possibility is looking pretty dim," Egill confidently answered.

"We sail for Iceland in two days. Why start courting someone when you know you will be gone for six months?" Tor asked.

"I am sorry, Egill Hallundsson, but my servant is not available for courting at this time. Cairenn is too young, and I cannot have her head full of thoughts about sailors. She has too many duties in this hall. Thank you for carrying the rice. I can give you a loaf of bread or a round of cheese for your trouble, but I cannot allow you to court my servant." Hryn's voice told Egill he would get nowhere in arguing his case in this hall.

"No payment is needed. It was a pleasure talking with you today, Cairenn, Heidi." Egill nodded and turned to the door. Cairenn's face was redder than her hair. Heidi's eyes betrayed her disappointment.

After Egill left, Hryn took Cairenn over by the hearth and talked quietly with her. Tor took Heidi and Erik over to their bed and quietly asked, "What happened? Tell me everything."

Heidi told the story but left out the insults that people at the trader booths directed at her. "I was surprised that Egill stood up for us and was so polite. I think he is smitten with Cairenn. It is almost sad that Hryn will not allow Egill to call on her."

"No, it is not sad. It is practical. There is too

much work here for Hryn to handle by herself, and he will always be gone for most of the year," Tor replied.

"Says the man who fell in love with a woman he could not even talk to." She smiled demurely at him as she studied his reaction.

"My hungry!" Erik interrupted, looking up and around his mother's growing belly.

Tor smiled and picked him up while Heidi went to get him a piece of bread with honey drizzled on it.

"Excuse me, I just need to get Erik some bread," she interrupted Hryn and Cairenn. Hryn had a stern but sad look on her face, while Cairenn was obviously crying. Heidi remembered trying to talk *Pena* out of falling in love with *Bud. How foolish to think that one can reason with love!* She shook her head and rejoined her husband and son.

Conversation at the dinner table that evening was subdued and very limited. Hryn looked past everyone while Cairenn just looked at her bowl. She barely touched her food and only answered yes and no questions. Tor and Heidi occupied themselves with Erik.

The next day, Tor went down to help Bjarni's crew get the ship rigged and ready for the four-day voyage to Iceland. They would carry no livestock, but had several bales of Greenlandic wool, bundles of ice bear, walrus, seal, and caribou hides, along with barrels filled with seal and walrus oil, walrus ivory, narwhal tusks, whale teeth, bear teeth, bear claws, and two complete bear skulls. Fifteen of the twenty-five logs they brought back from Vinland would stay in Brattahlid, so the raft was reduced to just ten logs.

Tor noted that when they took a break about midmorning, Egill did not return. He had to wonder if Cairenn was missing at that same time. By midafternoon, Egill was back working as if he had never been gone. Egill avoided Tor, so no questions were asked.

That night Tor noted that Cairenn was in much better spirits, even laughed a couple of times. When time and privacy allowed, Heidi confided that she occupied Hryn at the loom while Cairenn ran errands.

———

AT FIRST LIGHT on the fourth day after arriving at Brattahlid, Thorkell's ship, with Bjarni at the steerboard pushed away from the dock loaded for Iceland. On the shore, Hryn stoically stood with her arms crossed, praying for the soul of the Skræling girl who became a part of her life in a few short days. Next to her stood a young Irish servant girl who held tears in her eyes for a bearded sailor who promised to come back next spring before sailing for Vinland to look for a new place to trade wool for logs. Little did any of them know that new life was started in the young girl's womb.

Heidi and Erik vigorously waved goodbye from the rear deck behind the steerboard. Tor was busy pulling on an oar while Bjarni steered them down the fjord toward the sea and a new home.

CHAPTER 17

VISITORS

Cairenn busied herself preparing rice and some greens to put in a stew while Hryn sliced up a fresh cod that Hryn found at the trader booths earlier in the morning. Suddenly a hand pounded on the door to Hryn's modest hall.

Cairenn dropped her knife, wiped her hands, and went to the door. She opened the door a crack to see Father Harold, an attendant, and a man named Bjorn, representative of the court of Leif Eriksson, Lord of Brattahlid standing outside the door. Father Harald spoke first. "This is the home of Reginn Engarsson?"

"Y...yes," Cairenn replied shyly, looking down.

"And Hryn Reginnswife is in charge of the

household while Reginn Engarsson is away?" Father Harald demanded.

"Yes."

"Is Hryn Reginnswife in the hall?"

"Yes."

"Then let us in, we have questions for her." It was an order, not a request for permission. The three men walked past her while she held the door.

Hryn was busy washing the smell of cod from her hands and trying to look presentable to nobility all at once. Bjorn spoke up first. "Please excuse our intrusion into your home, Hryn Reginnswife. I am sure you are acquainted with Father Harald, and this is one of Leif Eriksson's squires." He indicated the young man standing behind him. "This morning, we received information that a Skræling was hiding in your hall. I wish to make the acquaintance of this Skræling, that I may ask questions of him."

The priest interjected, "You do know, Hryn, that it is improper and against Church law to harbor heathens in Christian homes? I have known you from the congregation these past several years and know that you hold a Christian home."

"They arrived on Thorkell Rolfcarlsson's ship, mastered by Bjarni Einarrsson five days past. The crowd was yelling insults at the young man and woman, who held a babe of mixed race on her hip, and another in her womb. I felt the Christian thing to do was to offer them shelter for the short time they were here.

"Bjarni sailed for Iceland yesterday, on the tide. The man claimed he was a Norwegian, ship-wrecked more than ten years past. He was the only survivor of two ships sailing for Greenland. His name is Tor Eriksson and claims to be a nephew of Thorkell Rolfcarlsson. With his blue eyes and blond hair, he is no Skræling.

"They sailed with Bjarni to Borgarnes to find Thorkell. The young woman was named Heidr Tungl*l*, which I shortened to 'Heidi.' She was pleased with the sound of that name and adopted it immediately. Amazingly, she could speak Norse with little difficulty. Tor claimed that they were married according to the customs and rites of her world, and that as soon as they came to a stop in their journey, she would convert to Christianity, and they would be married properly as Christians. It is a shame that you missed them. They were both intelligent and caring people.

"Though, I do fear for her soul, father. She has killed men in her past, and though she said she would accept and love the Christian God, she would not denounce the heathen gods she had known her entire life. She claimed that one of those 'gods' guided her through times of great danger. I rather think that God Almighty guided her for reasons unknown to us mortals."

"The woman is blasphemous and must be punished under Christian law!" Father Harald had no give in his shrill voice.

"She is out of our jurisdiction now, Father Harald," Bjorn said calmly, then turned to Hryn. "Did this Tor or Heidi mention *Hvitra-mannaland?*"

She shrugged her shoulders like she did not understand the question.

"Did he mention, or talk about a place called *Hvitramannaland*, or *White-men's Land*, or possibly *Greater Ireland?*"

"No, he made no mention of those places," Hryn replied.

"Was there any mention of white- or pale-skinned men?" Bjorn pressed.

"None that I can recall. Cairenn, did Heidi mention any of these things to you?" She turned to Cairenn, who stood behind her with her eyes studying the floor in front of her and her hands clenched tightly in front of her thighs.

"Heidi said that before she saw Tor, she had never heard of a white-skinned man. Her people did have myths about gods with white skin and yellow hair, but none really existed...until Tor, who they called *Yellow Hair,* came along," Cairenn answered nervously.

"It is a shame you did not get here in time to talk to them. They were a very friendly couple, and their young son was very active, but polite. I am sure they would answer all your questions," Hryn said sympathetically to Bjorn.

"You should have brought the heathens to the church immediately, Hryn. I am very disappointed in you. Your status in the Church is diminished by your lack of respect for the authority vested in it," Father Harald reprimanded her.

"Father, I was certainly not aware of such church laws, and the subject people were only passing through. Their purpose was to get to Iceland. Poor Tor had seen his entire family die in front of his eyes and was castaway in a foreign land. He did the best he could. He came of age in that strange land and met Heidi who had suffered her own trials. Naturally they were attracted to each other and married under the conditions of the place they found themselves in. I only tried to shelter them from the hatred the locals were suffering upon them. I am sorry if I committed some sin, but I thought I was showing kindness to those in need, as Jesus Christ himself espoused." Hryn answered back sharply. Cairenn's face turned bright red.

Father Harald started to say something else when Bjorn cut him off, saying, "What is done is done, Father. Do not be too harsh on the woman for doing what she saw as righteous. I do pray that they will find their home in Iceland and live a holy life. I just wish I could have gleaned more information from them. If we could find a way to deal with the Skræling on friendly terms, perhaps many of them would convert to Christianity and become strong partners with Greenland."

"Do not get your hopes up, my lord. Those Skræling are not recognized in the scriptures. God left them out of his world for a reason. No good will ever come out of their world." Father Harald was adamant.

"Hryn, is there anything more that you or your servant can recall that they said about Vinland and the Skræling living there?" Bjorn asked politely.

"My lord, Tor was very adamant that the Skræling were people, nothing less. They may have different beliefs and live lives differently than us, but they are people, nonetheless. He did mention that one group of them is building a city larger than any he knows of, perhaps excepting Rome. The people are building mountains from clay, sand, and dirt. They erect great temples on these manmade mountains to be closer to their sky gods, as I understood his meaning."

"Blasphemy, idol worship! God will punish them," Father Harald exclaimed.

"Or simple ignorance. Many of our pagan Norsemen converted as soon as they heard the Word," Bjorn mused.

"Yes, and many converted at the point of a sword!" Harald snapped back.

"Come, we have taken enough of Hryn's time," Bjorn said, then turned to Hryn. "If they should return to our shores and your abode, please contact my lord, Leif Eriksson, by any means you have."

"I will, my lord," Hryn replied and bowed her head toward him.

CHAPTER 18

LAST VOYAGE

By the end of the third day out from Brattahlid, a crewmember shouted he could see the sun shining off the ice and snow covered peaks of Iceland. A shout of joy went up. Married men would see their wives the next day after six months at sea or on strange shores. The single men knew where the best mead was to be found and the most willing maidens.

Tor was filled with apprehension. What would he say to Thorkell? Would the old man even recognize him? Probably not.

At first light the following morning, Iceland loomed large in front of them. As soon as everyone took care of their morning business and the sailors were in position to take up oars when they approached the port of Borg on Borgarnes, Tor came on deck and stood before them.

"To the men of this ship, I wish to thank each and every one of you for delivering me back to my family. In payment for your loyalty to my uncle, to Shipmaster Bjarni, and to me, I have payment for you. Come forward one at a time and receive payment of two silver nuggets. These nuggets originated in the great Shining Mountains, far in the west of Turtle Island. I never saw those mountains but listened to some who had. They sound truly magnificent, like those running down the spine of Norway. Traders from those mountains brought these nuggets to the city of Cahokia where my partner and I traded for them. The people there make jewelry out of them. You can do as you wish. I know this silver is of the highest quality and purity of any in the known world. I hope you find good use for them."

After each man had come forward and received his two nuggets, Tor turned to Bjarni. "To Bjarni, I offer a single nugget of a slightly different size." Tor reached into his bag and pulled out a nugget of pure silver nearly as big as a man's fist. It weighed half a stone.

"This is worth half a ship, are you sure you want to part with it?" Bjarni stared at the hunk of bright silver in his hand.

"It is yours, Shipmaster." Tor hugged Bjarni, then said, "Now, can we get landed so I can find my uncle?"

"Sail men, prepare to lower the sail! Oarsmen, place oars!" Bjarni called out as he slid the big silver nugget in his waist pouch.

As the ship came to a stop alongside a wooden dock, Bjarni turned to Tor and said, "Get your family and come with me."

"Where?"

"You will see soon enough. My men will bring your belongings." Bjarni smiled. *Either I have been played for a fool, or this is going to be an emotional episode.*

At the top of the rise leading up from the docks was a flat square where town folk sold their wares and traded news, especially when a ship docked. From Bjarni's horn signal, they knew it was him returning from Vinland. The news would not be exciting. Ships from Norway always had exciting news, but from Vinland, unless the Skræling had killed someone, there would not be much to talk about. Thorkell sat on his great horse, Thunder, and waited for Bjarni to break over the rise with a report on the trading.

To Thorkell's surprise, three figures strode up the road from the docks. *Who comes with Bjarni? A big man, dressed like a Skræling, he has a child in his arms. And a woman walks with them, she is with child. She is a Skræling! Bjarni best have a good explanation for this. Thralls, gifts for me? The man has Norse hair and features. Something familiar about him...* He dismounted and stood with a hand on the saddle to stead his wobbly legs. "Bjarni!..." he called out. *That face...he looks like...*

"Thorkell, my lord, I have someone for you to meet." Bjarni smiled.

Suddenly, Thorkell's eyes filled with tears. Heidi glanced at Tor. His eyes were filled with tears as well. She studied the two men as they studied each other. *The recognition is obvious. Thorkell is slightly smaller than Tor, but he is an elder. His head of thinning hair and beard are silver-gray. But his clothes are neat and well made. He stands trembling.*

"My lord, this man claims to be *Tor Eriksson,* a relative of yours."

"Yes, yes." Thorkell stuttered, "I...I thought my entire family was lost to me. A miracle from God has descended upon me." He wept as his old knees failed him. Bjarni and Tor stepped in and caught him before he went down. They lifted him back to his feet. Tor handed Erik to the woman and bear-hugged him, speechless, tears flooding both men's faces. "H...how?" Thorkell asked into Tor's ear.

"The story is a long one, uncle. Perhaps we

should retire to your hall. I must introduce you to my family," Tor said proudly.

"Family?" Thorkell questioned, surprise in his voice. His mind muddled by the circumstances, he blurted, "You probably do not know, but marriage of Norse to Skræling is forbidden, especially in a family of our standing. And holding slaves in this district is greatly frowned upon. We will have to arrange for Bjarni to take her back to her people in the spring."

"We will talk about this another time, Uncle, but know that she is no Skræling. In fact, none of them are. Let me introduce her. Uncle Thorkell, this is Heidr Tungl Torswife. She was given a shortened version, Heidi, by a friend. The boy is Erik Torsson, named after my late father. As you can see, another will be born in the coming winter. Heidi, this is the uncle you have heard so much about. He is Thorkell Rolfcarlsson."

She held out a hand to the old man, curtsied slightly, and said, "It is a pleasure to make the acquaintance of such a powerful elder." She quoted the line she had rehearsed in her head a thousand times. She felt the perspiration burning her wet armpits.

He took her hand and reluctantly kissed it. "The pleasure is mine," he said politely to her, surprised at her ability to speak Norse. He patted the boy on the head, then turned to Tor and said, "My, but she is a beauty. You are full of surprises, Tor Eriksson."

A couple of the sailors, as per Bjarni's instruction, came up the road with Tor and Heidi's belongings.

"We should start for Rolfcarlslandstedr. It is a long walk," Thorkell said, then added, "Bjarni, help me mount Thunder, please."

Bjarni started forward, but Tor stepped in and said, "Allow me, Uncle, I insist."

When Thorkell was seated on his great horse, Tor patted the animal's neck, a tear leaked from his eye and trickled down his cheek. "I have not touched a horse since I was a boy," he said to no one. "Uncle, I have so much to tell you." He looked up through bleary eyes to the man in the saddle.

"And I you, my boy," Thorkell answered, a touch of sadness in his hoarse voice.

CHAPTER 19

ROLFCARLSLANDSTEDR

As they walked along, Thorkell explained the circumstances that brought him and his wife to Iceland. "The farm and hall here were built by Hrolfr Laugardair, my wife's father. It was known as Laugardairslandstedr. My wife, Hildr, was the youngest of six, and the only one still living. Shortly after your voyage began, Hrolfr's wife, Hlin, died. In four summers, he passed as well. Shortly after that, a man named Jalfadr Hallgardrsson came to my farm in the Western Settlement and offered me a hoard of silver for it. Hildr and I discussed it and decided all we worked for there came to naught. Our only children, our sons, had been taken from us. Her brothers and their families, who had established farms near ours, died in accidents or of diseases. Then, your families were lost at sea. No one was left for us to pass the farm on to. So, we sold it, dug up our sons' bones, and brought them here. We were at a loss for what to do with this farm since we had no family left. It looked as though I would have to give it to the King of Norway or maybe the Church. All that has changed now. Of course, it will be yours when Hildr and I are finished on this earth."

"You still have family in Norway, Uncle. There is Svein and his children, and the children of Lokhilla," Tor replied.

"There is no good news for you from Norway, I am afraid, Tor. And no good way to tell you," Thorkell started.

Tor froze in his tracks and looked at Thorkell. Fear shone on his face. Heidi looked at Tor and wanted to go and comfort him in any way she could.

"Lokhilla remarried within the year after you left Ulfrstadt. Her husband was a strong warrior. He won much glory in Northumbria and Mercia. He was in Ulfrstadt after a raid and drank far too much, I am told. In his stupor, somehow, he managed to catch the hall my brother built on fire. All were lost—him, Lokhilla, her daughter and son-in-law, and their three children, along with three thralls, were all sound asleep and could not get out of the burning hall.

"That same summer, your uncle, Svein, was thrown from a horse he was breaking to saddle. He hit his head on a post and died instantly—in the same pen my brother was kicked in the head, which led to his death. After a period of mourning, Dagna married a suitor from Bergan. I believe he is a distant cousin to your mother. For the Yule celebration, Dagna and her family sailed down the coast to Bergen. Dagna's husband stayed in Bergen for some business dealings after the Yule celebrations while Dagna and her two children went back to Ulfrstadt. It is speculated that Dagna was carrying a child by her new husband. They were overtaken by a sudden storm in Ulfrfjord and capsized. All were lost, I am afraid. Dagna's husband said that the Rolfcarl clan was cursed by God and had the hall and all the outbuildings raised. He has since remarried and built a new hall and sheds. All traces of your family in Ulfrstadt have been erased except the burial plots of those who died there. It hurts to report these terrible things to you." Tears flowed freely down the old man's cheeks into his beard.

Erik said to Heidi, "Why is my mother crying? Is me too heavy?"

She hugged him tightly and replied, "No, my

little man, I am just sad about what the grandfather is telling your father."

By the time Thorkell's sad news was conveyed, his hall loomed in front of them. For the next three fingers of time, the party moved along the cart track in silence. The weather was fair, but clouds to the northwest signaled that a change was coming.

The countryside was in its autumn glory. The grasses and small trees were a mixture from light green to golden yellow. Summer barley fields and patches of grasses had been cut and put up for the winter. Horses, sheep, and cattle grazed leisurely in tall grass. The higher hills and distant mountains were covered with the first snow and ice of the coming winter. To the east and south, white steam and black smoke drifted skyward from an unseen volcano.

The hall was longer than any longhouse Heidi had ever seen. It rivaled Leif Eriksson's great hall in Brattahlid, which she had only seen from a distance. She studied the squat building with a low stone wall foundation topped with short logs arranged in a zigzag pattern to about shoulder high. Between the logs was a mud mixture with thick sod growing in it. The eaves overlapped the walls, and the roof was covered with thick, growing grass. Four rock chimneys protruded from the roof, and light-blue smoke drifted from each one. The biggest chimney, on the east end of the hall, released a thicker trail of smoke.

They approached from the south side. In the center of the long south wall was a wood-faced gable protruding from the growing sod edifice. The wooden gable stood over a wooden wall twice as tall as a man and featuring a large wooden door with flowers and spirals carved in it. Above the gable, the face boards were old ship keel boards crossed at the peak and running to the lower ends of the gable. The face boards were intricately carved with dragons and filigree.

They stopped in front of the gable, where two large posts stood as high as the gable and off to the east side. The posts were carved with spirals, flowers, geometric designs, some filigree, and topped with new crosses. The old dragon head tops had been removed and replaced to indicate this was now a Christian home. A smaller cross rail was attached between the two posts and served as a place to tie horse leads for visitors. Two young men ran from around the west end of the building and greeted Thorkell. They helped him down from the horse and led it back where they had come from.

"Come in," Thorkell said as he opened the great door and waved them all into the hall.

Inside was a great room divided between a kitchen on the east side and tables with chairs and benches filling the west part. At the west end of the great hall, a solid wooden wall separated space from the rest of the building. Sleeping benches lined the outside walls, making bed platforms for more than three tens of people. A large door in the center of that wall was closed. Six fat wooden posts supported thick wood beams about a man and a half high above a flat rock slab floor. The rock slabs had been polished smooth by foot traffic. The ceiling pitched at a low angle above the beams to the peak, which ran east and west down the center of the room. The outside walls were not quite head high to a man standing up. The walls were covered with flat boards fitted closely together, various pegs and spikes protruding to hang things on. Oil lamps hung from the heavy beams. Even so, it was somewhat dark in the room.

It looks much bigger from the outside. This will take some getting used to. It is like a cave, Heidi thought.

There were two doors along the back wall. One led to a storage area just off the kitchen. Through the storage area was another door that led to a dairy where cows and goats were milked and sour cream and cheeses made. The other door led to an indoor privy with seats and a flowing channel that washed waste to the outside, where it was collected to be used in fields and gardens for fertilizer. Hanging on the walls were things like snowshoes and rods for catching fish. There were pairs of flat boards that looked to have a place to put a foot. A leather strap looped from the middle of that spot, and the boards were as long as a man is tall, or more.

Must be for some game. Surely no one can walk with those tied to their feet, Heidi mused to herself. She noted one wall featured a tapestry that showed the family history from when Hildr and Thorkell were wed up till their move to Iceland.

Thorkell told Bjarni's men to carry Tor's belongings back to the second bedroom. When they had completed that, he told Bjarni that he should get back to the ship and report the news from Greenland and Vinland in the square so they could get back to the hall for the celebration of their successful voyage.

"Hungry, Mother," Erik said matter-of-factly. Heidi started to reach into her bag for a couple of cakes that she had left from the ones Cairenn gave her for the trip. They were getting quite stale.

When they entered the room, Hildr Thorkellswife was busy at a smooth flat rock slab that served as a workplace in the kitchen. It was worn baby-skin smooth by countless loaves of bread, cakes, pies, cobblers, and other food preparation tasks performed over the fifty years since it had been installed. She turned and was shocked to see the strangers enter her house. She looked at Thorkell with a million questions lying behind her eyes.

He saw and read the questions in her head before she opened her mouth. "Joy has come back into our lives this day, my love." Thorkell smiled at her as he spoke.

"You will have to explain a little further, husband," she replied, not quite as warmly as he had spoken to her.

"My dear, I want you to meet Tor Eriksson, come back from the dead, all the way from Vinland and beyond," he said cheerily.

She put her hands to her wrinkled cheeks, opened her mouth wide and found her chair. She plopped down hard in the chair, looking hard at Tor, tears already flowing freely from her half-lidded eyes. "Do not even make jokes about the dead!" she exclaimed, eyes turning red. *He looks exactly like Gunnar would look at his age!* she thought, as emotion overwhelmed her. Thorkell walked over and put his arm over her shoulders.

"It is true, after all these years, Tor has found his way to us. And brought a wife and family, too. We will have to meet with Father Halnar about that, as she is of Skræling heritage." Now his tears started to flow again.

"Where have you been all this time, Tor?" Hildr asked between sobs.

"Me hungry!" Erik exclaimed.

"Of course, you are, and you talk so well for such a little man! What is your name?"

Hildr struggled to her feet, hobbled over, and opened a ceramic crock on her big flat countertop and pulled out some flat cakes. Then she reached up on a shelf and took down a small ceramic jar with a little wood stick in it. She put the cakes on a small wood plate and pulled the stick from the jar. The stick flared out to a knuckle width and made round with slots cut in it. With that, she dribbled honey all over the cakes and took them to the table and indicated for Heidi to sit with the boy on a bench so he could eat his cakes.

When he said "Erik," she almost dropped the honey dipper. She looked at Thorkell and said, "Are you going to introduce these people, or just let them introduce themselves, old man?"

"Of course, where are my manners? I am sorry, just a bit overwhelmed right now. My dear, as I said, this is Tor Eriksson, the son of our nephew, who is no longer with us. And this young woman is Heidi Torswife, and you have already met little Erik Torsson. As you can see, Heidi will be bringing another child into our lives in a few months." Thorkell tried not to sound too emotional.

"I am very pleased to meet you, Hildr Thorkell-swife." Heidi smiled.

Hildr looked at Tor and asked, "How?" as she shook her head, still in disbelief.

Tow was not sure what question she was asking. "Aunt, our stories are long, with many twists and turns, but how about I tell you what led us to Iceland?" She nodded as she sat back in her chair. Thorkell settled into his chair, his full attention on Tor.

"We were in the great, growing city of Cahokia, on the Grandfather River. I will explain how we got there at a later time. Heidi, who was known at that time as Bright Moon, *Heidr Tungl*, was temporarily separated from me. I was with a friend who had led us to Cahokia. He was a trader and traveled far and wide over much of *Turtle Island*. I will explain that later as well. When I joined him among the other traders, one who I had met more than a year earlier, said he had something to show me. We went to his packs, and he pulled out a woolen hat. One made in Greenland by Uncle Thorkell's thralls. I was sure I recognized the pattern and the weave. Naturally, I asked where he got it. The trader told me he knew I would be interested.

"To make a long story short, he guided us up

and down many rivers until he introduced us to another trader who could bring me to the Micmac people. Erik had been born by this time. The Micmac people are the ones who were trading their forest trees for Thorkell's hats and red wool cloth. We got there in time to meet up with Bjarni and sail here! God wanted us to come back here."

Heidi grinned her approval and added, "Hardly that simple, husband, but well said."

"Would you care to tell us how you came to be married? I did not know God had priests in Vinland to perform marriages," Hildr asked innocently.

"I think it would be better to start with when we left Ulfrstadt and all the things that led up to that joyous time," Tor spoke nervously.

Hildr looked questioningly at Thorkell, who said quietly, "Let them tell their stories as they see fit, dear. Should the cook be in here working on the evening meal?"

"I think all the help went down to hear the news from Vinland and Brattahlid. They should be back soon and bring all of Bjarni's men and a few wives with them. All right, Tor, start from the beginning."

By the time Tor got to the first storm, a man came in with a large chunk of meat that had been cooking in a pit fire and smelled delicious. "We like to give the crew a celebration when they return from a voyage. We got word yesterday that some lookouts spotted the ship coming from the west." Thorkell smiled. "We expect they have eaten enough fish for a while. Are you ready for some beef?"

"We ate the oxen and sheep at the celebration when we left the Micmac. We have had turkey, grouse, deer, bear, elk, moose, and buffalo very much, along with assorted small animals, birds, fish, and insects. We *are* ready for some beef!"

"There is mead for the crew when they get here. Have you had that?" Thorkell asked.

"We had a few kegs when we left Ulfrstadt. Some of it was lost at sea, but we drank some. I was young—twelve, I believe. I have had black drink since then. Many of the people of Turtle Island make their own version of black drink. It has a similar effect as mead but tastes much differ-ent," Tor replied.

Thorkell looked at Hildr and smiled sheep-ishly. She nodded slightly. He got up and went through the small door in the north wall next to the kitchen. After several heartbeats, voices were heard and soon a big man came up the hall carrying a small barrel with a wooden plug in the end. The keg was opened, and the adults had a mug of mead while Erik was given a cup of cow's cream. After a taste of the mead, Heidi wanted tea.

Soon the hall was alive with Bjarni's crew members. The talk was loud, as was the laughter. Erik ran around the room giggling with crew members he had befriended on the ship. The few men who had wives in town brought them. At first, they were reluctant to even meet Heidi, but as the night wore on and the drink flowed, some warmed up to her and found out she was no evil demon after all. The single men did not consider her married since she was 'nothing but a Skræling,' but they remembered Egill's broken nose and kept their distance.

The celebration lasted well into the night. Sailing, fishing, and hunting songs and ditties floated around the room as soon as Egill brought out his small, stringed instrument and started strumming notes and telling sagas. Heidi felt she did the right thing by distracting Hryn so that Egill and Cairenn could get together. Perhaps Hryn would have a change of mind by the time Bjarni set sail for Brattahlid in the spring.

CHAPTER 20

GERNA

Over the next several weeks, the weather changed drastically as winter set in. Gradually Tor and Heidi shared many of their stories. Heidi soon learned what the long flat boards with foot straps were for. Even in her awkward, pregnant state, she was able to use the skis on flat ground without falling.

Hildr saw to it that Tor and Heidi were acquainted with Father Halnar. He began lessons to convert Heidi to Christianity. He was happy to convert her, but said, "Let it be known, in no uncertain terms, that Tor and Heidi are sinners."

Tor attended the classes because he felt he needed them as much as she did. When the lessons got to the part about forsaking all other gods and denigrating the Skræling for being heathen, there were problems. Father Halnar was schooled as much as his pupils. He walked out in anger on several occasions and even told Hildr that the case was hopeless. Each time, she talked him into reconsidering and trying a different approach.

In the end, Father Halnar decided he could slowly work those parts into their ideology over a long period of time. He readily baptized Erik but refused to do the same with Heidi. He even threatened Tor with excommunication.

After the Yule, the issue still was not resolved. Making his point stronger, Father Halnar refused to meet with Tor and Heidi at the same time. His reasoning was that he could wear them down one-on-one, while together, their resistance to his arguments would be stronger. He was wrong.

———

OVER THE WINTER, Thorkell and Tor had serious discussions about the future. Thorkell said he wanted Tor and his family to stay on the farm. They were his only heirs and wanted to keep it in the family. Tor insisted that he and Heidi needed to make their own way in the world.

In the end, Thorkell won the argument, and it was agreed that Tor would gradually take over the management of the holdings. Thorkell apologized to Tor that he had promised his ship to Bjarni and saw no way that he could undo that decision.

Tor told Thorkell about his dream of opening a trade liaison with the peoples of Turtle Island. Thorkell advised Tor that it would be most difficult to change Norse attitudes toward the people they regarded as less than human. "The Church will see it as their duty to convert all those friends of yours to Christianity—by force if necessary. How do you think that will work out? I think your ideas are good ones, but I cannot see Norsemen giving those people the respect they, and you, seem to think they deserve. I see only conflict. I am sorry."

"Uncle, we just have to have one successful voyage to show that trading with them could be prosperous," Tor pleaded.

"And what crew do you suppose would sail to these unknown waters with you? Can you find forty men who feel as you do? I rather doubt it." Thorkell's words were like pouring water on red coals. Tor saw his dreams dissipating like steam. *I should never have taken Bright Moon from her world,* he brooded.

"Perhaps you can discuss it with Bjarni. He is younger than me, he may see it differently." Thorkell gave Tor a ray of hope.

In the meantime, Heidi learned to make cloth on Hildr's loom. Heidi argued with Hildr that tanned skins with the hair left on made better cold-weather clothes than wool. Hildr calmly argued that skin clothes were for heathens and warriors, not civilized Christians.

———

Toward the end of the hard winter, Heidi woke up one morning and felt like she had to milk the four cows, all six goats, carry the milk to the holding tanks, feed the horses, churn butter, chop kindling, and wash the bedding, all before breakfast. Hildr just let her go. In fact, she had her haul in extra water and get it heated up in the big kitchen fireplace. Hildr then let Heidi go about her work while she quietly got a spare bedroom ready for the birth of the baby she knew would be coming that afternoon. She sent one of the house servants to get Skulda Leikskalarswife to help with the birth. She was the best midwife Hildr knew. By midday, Heidi sat down, exhausted. Within a hand of time, she began to feel the birth pains coming.

Unlike Erik's coming into the world, the birth of Gerna Torsdottir came easy for Heidi. The child was well positioned, and Heidi's strong core muscles pushed her out smoothly after only six hands of time from her first pain. Gerna's skin was pink and healthy, and she cried loud and strong.

Within days, Heidi was back in her normal routine, doing the work of two women, and even joining in with men's chores.

Heidi loved taking care of the animals. In her world, save a few dogs that were largely ignored, all the animals were wild and mainly used for food, their hides and some of their bones for tools. Here she could touch and talk to the tame animals. She quickly learned to milk the goats and cows. Before Gerna was born, Tor would not allow her to ride a horse, but within a month after Gerna's birth, Heidi was riding a horse every day with the baby strapped into a cradleboard on her back and bundled against the cold.

———

FATHER HALNAR CONTINUED his Christian lessons with Heidi into the spring. He insisted that Heidi cover up with a shawl while Gerna was nursing. As time wore on, he adopted an increasingly friendly tone. She responded kindly. One fine spring morning, they sat in the rectory discussing the Creator Spirit from Heidi's world. She insisted how similar that spirit was to the Christian God. She wore an ankle-length, light blue-colored, thin wool dress.

At some point in the discussion, he smiled, leaned toward her, and put his hand under her hem, and up to her knee. Then started to slide it up the inside of her thigh, under her dress. Before he could even blink, her hand gripped his wrist so tightly he could feel the bones grating together. "Your god commands that 'Thou shall not covet thy neighbor's wife!'" she growled through clenched teeth.

"But, Heidi, your tone has been one of acceptance of late. I took your actions as an invitation. And remember, you are not yet baptized. You are still a heathen and cannot be a real wife. You are hurting my wrist. I insist you let go." His voice began to quiver as she gripped harder.

"I will let go when you apologize for your transgression and swear by God Almighty that you will never do anything like this again, to me or any other woman. Swear it!" she insisted.

"My actions are none of your affair, and I will not apologize to a heathen." His voice was more of a whimper.

"Swear it!" She squeezed even harder.

He dropped to his knees. "I swear," he cried, tears trickling from the corners of his eyes.

She relaxed her grip but did not let go. "Now, you will perform the baptism rite for me on Sabbath next. And you will speak with Tor about performing our Christian wedding. Are we in agreement?" Her voice was calm, but she let him know she still had a grip on his throbbing wrist.

He nodded and looked at the floor. She released his wrist and turned to walk out. Over her shoulder, she said with a smile, "I will tell Tor and Hildr about the baptism and help prepare a feast for after the services at Rolfcarlslandstedr. You will come and say nothing other than you and I have come to an understanding, and I have earned the right to be baptized in the Christian Church. Am I right?"

"You are right." He looked down, humiliated, as he rubbed his aching wrist.

The baptism and feast went according to Heidi's wishes for the most part. Father Halnar did have a talk with Tor in which he said quietly, "Heidi is a strong-willed woman. Are you sure you want her as your wife? She may not be as subservient as a good wife should be."

"I am sure, Father. Her will is her strength, and without her strength, I would not be here today," Tor replied evenly.

"Very well. Shall we talk about a Christian wedding?"

"Yes!" Tor beamed.

At the wedding feast, Egill made a moment to talk to Heidi alone while Hildr paraded around showing the women her "granddaughter." "Do you think Cairenn will remember me? We sail for Brattahlid in three days. I have decided I want to ask for her hand in marriage. Do you think Hryn will grant it?"

"I cannot speak for Hryn, but I am sure Cairenn remembers you well. I have no doubt that she loves you. Do you have a bride-price to offer?"

"I have a small hoard of silver and an ivory crucifix I carved over this past winter," Egill replied eagerly.

"I suspect the crucifix will come closer to winning Hryn's heart than the silver. Maybe you should save that for your household. Or, if the crucifix is not enough for Hryn, you can offer at least some of it. I want you to be sure to tell Hryn that I was baptized, and that Tor is now my Christian husband. And do not forget that Gerna was born healthy. I have many things to tell her. I wish I could see her. One day, Tor and I will sail to visit her. Tell her that." Heidi was almost giddy.

"I will, Heidi." He pointed to his crooked nose and said, "I owe you much."

She smiled, then was interrupted by a hungry Gerna. Egill walked away with a smile on his face and went toward the mead table.

Gerna, now three months old, had developed large, deep-brown eyes, the high cheekbones of Heidi's beautiful face, and what little hair she had was dark brown and stood out straight like pinfeathers on a baby duck. Her skin was still a light pink, like a Norse baby. As she eagerly suckled her full breast. Heidi thought sadly, *had we wintered in the Micmac village, Bull Moose would have killed the baby for having Yellow Hair's skin.* She shook sadness from her head as she watched her daughter feed.

"What did he want?" Tor asked sternly as he slipped up behind her.

Cooing to Gerna, she turned her head and asked, "Who?" Her thoughts were only on Gerna and how she would grow up so differently than Heidi had.

"Egill. I suppose he wants an unholy alliance with you," Tor said crossly.

She smiled. "Jealousy does not become you, husband. He was asking me about marrying Cairenn when they get to Brattahlid. I told him Hryn will expect a bride-price."

"Oh," he said quietly. "I think Hryn will not allow Cairenn to be married to a seaman. I hope I am wrong. Egill is a good man at heart, just a little misguided at times." As he gripped her bottom.

"Careful," she said, "I would not want to mess up your pretty face!"

"When Gerna sleeps tonight, we will consummate our marriage the right way." He smiled, glad that his bright blue wedding tunic covered his bulging manhood.

She smiled coyly and said in husky tone, "I promise, husband."

The following day, Tor and Thorkell made arrangements to petition the Godi to allow Heidi and all her descendants to become full citizens of Iceland based on the fact that Tor and Heidi were married in Vinland before Tor had any knowledge of any law forbidding their marriage. The Godi said the matter would be settled by the entire Gothi at the Althing in the summer.

CHAPTER 21

EGILL AND CAIRENN

When Bjarni's ship landed in Brattahlid, Hryn waited for Egill to come up the street from the dock, but Cairenn was nowhere in sight. His heart sank. But he had to know if Cairenn had married another, so he approached Hryn.

"About time you showed up, you worthless piece of human flotsam!" Hryn called out when he was still several paces away.

"What have I done, Hryn Reginnswife?" His heart pounding in his chest.

"You know as well as you are standing there what you did. And no word from you all winter? Do you think she wants to have that child with no father? What is wrong with you?" Her tongue was wound up and would not stop throwing insults at him. "How many other bastard children and husbandless mothers have you left behind?"

"Hryn, Hryn, I know not what you are saying. Is Cairenn with child? Could it be mine? Oh, blessed are the saints! I was coming to ask her hand in marriage. But I know nothing of a child," Egill stammered.

"That is right, you know nothing. God gave you that worm to make babies, not satisfy your own lust. What did you think would happen when you planted your worthless seed in that poor, innocent girl? You should be castrated and hung in the square!

"But then if you are willing to make an honest, Christian wife of her...I suppose...but what of your life? You are always at sea. No life for a young mother."

She thought of her own life. Married to a man of the sea. Only home long enough to get her pregnant, then help bury the child a year or two later. Their three children had been born sickly. Only one lived more than a year, but little more. She did not want that for Cairenn. Cairenn was a wedding gift from her parents. Cairenn's mother had been their house servant in Norway before they moved to Iceland and then to Greenland. Cairenn was born in Greenland when Hryn was not yet a woman.

She felt complete responsibility for the humble, hardworking girl.

"No, you may not marry her as long as you belong to the sea. The sea is your mistress. I do know a shipwright in Gardar, however. I think he could use a hand. If you are worth your eagerness to bed my servant, you will seek local work and forgo your lust for the sea."

"Do you mean it, Hryn? I will gladly forsake the sea for Cairenn. She is the love of my life. But Bjarni has me under his power. How will I get out of that? Perhaps after this voyage to Vinland?" Egill questioned.

"This village and Gardar are crawling with young single men who want to go to sea, and some seasoned ones as well. I am sure Bjarni will have no issue replacing you. Now, go find employment and square with Bjarni before you come back to visit my house. And mind you, Reginn Engarsson has not yet sailed, you will be proper around Cairenn," Hryn admonished Egill.

"Thank you, thank you, thank you!" he shouted. He put his hand on her shoulder and turned back toward the dock.

Within a month, Egill and Cairenn were married and living in a tiny house close to Hryn's hall. Every day Egill took a ferry across Eriksfjord and walked the short distance to the shipwright's shipworks in Gardar. Cairenn continued her work as Hryn's housemaid. Her duties lessened as her pregnancy advanced to its final stages.

———

THE SCOUTS WATCHED the great canoe come to a stop a safe distance from shore. It was late at night, and Bjarni did not want to disturb Bull Moose at that hour. The ship settled into quiet stillness after the heavy anchor chain lowered the anchor stone to the bottom of the bay. Tomorrow Bjarni would bargain with Bull Moose for more trees. He took Tor's advice and brought more valuable trade goods that were sure to win the favor of Bull Moose.

After the Norsemen had settled into sleep, four dugout canoes approached in complete silence. Overcast skies helped hide the dark canoes sliding slowly across the dark water. When they pulled alongside, reed brushes were used to saturate the wood planks just above the waterline with boiled pine pitch. As soon as both sides of the ship were soaked, a warrior on each side opened a small ceramic container with hot coals in it. A torch dipped in pine tar was touched to the hot coals, then the flaming torch quickly slid down the length of the ship, igniting the smeared pine pith.

The hull of the ship was engulfed in flames while the canoes rapidly fled.

Bull Moose stood on the shore and watched the ship burn and listened to the screaming sailors as they jumped into the frigid waters of the bay. Only two Norsemen were able to make it to the shore alive, and they were shot many times with arrows, never getting out of the water. "Humph! I warned him not to return." Bull Moose scowled. Parts of the ship still smoldered at dawn as water seeped into the burned-out hull below the waterline. No word ever reached Greenland or Iceland as to the fate of Bjarni's final voyage to Vinland.

CHAPTER 22
INHERITANCE

One day in late May, Tor was working on a worn bridle when Thorkell tottered over to him, looked at his work, and said, "Fine job, Gunnar, you are becoming a man."

Stunned, Tor looked up and said, "Uncle, I am Tor."

Thorkell replied, "Yes, yes, of course." He had an odd, questioning look in his eye and a crooked smile. He just walked away into the hall.

"Are you feeling all right, uncle?" Tor called out to him. Thorkell did not look back, just turned his head slightly and raised his hand dismissively.

That night Tor talked it over with Hildr when Thorkell had fallen asleep in his chair. "You are just noticing?" she asked. "His mind has been slipping of late. His memory is failing. I fear his long life is coming to an end. It has been a good life, a bitter-sweet life. He has known great prosperity and tragic loss. He misses our sons more than words can tell. And I know being the last of the Rolf-carlsson brothers has torn him from within. Family has always meant so much to him." A tear trickled down her cheek.

As spring faded into summer and farm work intensified with the cutting and storing of hay, harvesting the self-sown rice ripening near the water, harvesting the sown barley, tending live-stock, Thorkell drew further and further into himself. Most times when he talked to people, he smiled, but was given to hateful bursts of bad temperament, especially in the late afternoon hours and particularly toward Erik and Hildr. With more and more frequency, he had difficulty remembering the smallest things. Oftentimes, he referred to Tor as Gunnar, his late son's name. He also began to wander aimlessly. His eyes lost their keen focus. Tor increasingly had to keep an eye on him when they were outside. On a couple of occasions, he was nearly to town before Tor caught up to him. "Just going to pick up the keel for a boat I am building," he told Tor on one such occasion.

Hildr cried herself to sleep late each night knowing her lifelong companion was slipping away from her. Lack of sleep and worry were taking their toll on her strong mind. Heidi spent her days trying to console and comfort the old woman. She had witnessed a few elders in her life who acted like Thorkell was. She recalled one instance where the man had no living relatives. He was given a bow and quiver, along with a flint knife, and allowed to wander off. No one ever saw him again. Sadness filled the hall that summer.

THORKELL MANAGED to attend the Althing with Tor and helped him present his case to the Gothi. In the end, the Lawspeaker declared that Tor and his wife had no prior knowledge of the law forbidding their marriage, therefore, the law did not apply, and Heidi Torswife and any descendants they had would be granted full Icelandic citizenship.

EARLY IN THE FALL, Thorkell slipped away from the watchful eyes of the family. Tor was butchering a cow, Erik was helping all his three-summers old body would allow, Heidi was tending to Gerna's needs, and Hildr was at her loom, lost in depression.

While Thorkell wandered across the hills, a cold rain blew in from the north. When they discovered that Thorkell was missing, Tor saddled a horse and went down the lane to find him. He got all the way to town and found no one who had seen him. Ice was beginning to form on the trees and other vegetation. Back at the hall, no one had found Thorkell yet.

Shivering in a small copse of birch trees, Thorkell tried to fathom where he was and how he got there. *Where is Mother? She would never leave me here with these strange people. They will not even talk to me. This is a fine mess. I will just wait for Mother. She'll be here soon.* "Harald? Where are you? Sigurd, is that you? I'm over here. Why can't you see me? Haakon will be here soon, he'll be mad!" Darkness started to descend on him. *Wish I had a sheep, they are always warm.* His addled brain could not make sense of anything.

All the farm help, a few people from Borg, and Tor were combing the countryside as darkness fell. The freezing rain continued into the night, making the search increasingly difficult. Their world turned into a silvery, dreamlike landscape. Every step was a crunch. The only sound was the falling rain that froze on contact, building a thicker and thicker coating on everything exposed. The searchers carried oil torches that sputtered and smoked but gave off a pitifully small amount of light. The search went on all night, and the searchers came up empty.

By dawn, the rain had stopped, but the temperature remained below freezing. Without sleep, Tor saddled the horse again and set out across the fields. He tried to think of Thorkell's favorite places on the farm. He remembered a little spring in a gully in the middle of a meadow. The spring was surrounded by a little copse of birch trees, and Thorkell said it produced the sweetest water in all of Iceland. It was more than three leagues from the hall, and Tor could not see how Thorkell would have gotten that far. He hoped against hope that someone in town had taken him in for the night.

Tor crested a hill and looked down on the little grove of trees. Somehow, he knew he would find Thorkell's body there. *What a lonely place for a great man to die,* he thought as he looked at the small trees bent from the heavy ice that clung to their branches. Tears streamed from Tor's eyes as he dismounted onto the crunchy grass next to the little trees. Thorkell's lifeless body sat propped against a small tree. Oddly, his face bore a crooked smile. *What was his last thought?* Tor cried as he lifted the stiff body. Tor was amazed at how light Thorkell had become. Nearly a year ago, when Tor arrived in Borg, Thorkell had been almost his size. Now he did not weigh half as much as he had then.

All of Borg turned out for Thorkell's funeral, and many tributes to him were spoken to Hildr and Tor at the feast in Rolfcarllandstedr Hall. Tor was amazed at the outpouring of tribute for a man who had only lived among them for six years. *He truly was a great man. Loved by all who knew him,* he proudly mused.

———

WINTER SET in with no word from Bjarni. Tor concluded that they had to go far to find a peaceful people to trade with. They must have had to overwinter there. He was convinced that the white, upturned hands painted on the bow of the ship and the variety of trade goods that he had talked Bjarni into taking would win Bjarni favor with some people of Vinland, perhaps even someone who had known of Yellow Hair and Bright Moon. He still held on to his dream of peaceful trade routes being established, maybe even a trip with him and his family someday among the peoples he had met.

Late in the winter, Hildr died in her sleep. She had a smile on her face when Heidi found her in bed. Another funeral followed by an outpouring of love and honor for the deceased filled the hall. After the hall emptied of the mourners, Tor and Heidi looked in on Erik and Gerna to find them sleeping peacefully. Heidi turned to Tor and said, "Sometimes when God takes a life, He gives a new one in its place." She held her hand on her belly and smiled. Tor hugged her. She felt a warm wetness on her cheek.

CHAPTER 23

TWINS

As the summer solstice approached, a ship arrived from Brattahlid. Tor, Heidi, and the children went to town to hear the news from Brattahlid. Perhaps there would be word of Bjarni. The first thing Heidi noticed was a woman in long, wavy, orange hair carrying a little girl with glowing red hair on her hip. Next to her was a plain-dressed big man carrying a large bag. "Any rooms for guests from Brattahlid on these shores?" The man smiled at Heidi as he talked.

"As long as I get to hold that beautiful child in my arms!" a very pregnant Heidi gushed.

"Granted!" Cairenn beamed, walked up, and plopped her child in Heidi's outstretched arms. The little girl did not even fuss. Tor and Egill hugged and exchanged pleasantries.

"What is your name?" Heidi asked.

The little girl dove her head into Heidi's neck, too shy to speak.

"Heidi Torswife, it would be my pleasure to introduce you to Heidi Hryn Egillsdottir," Cairenn announced. "I insisted we name her after the person who made her possible. And her middle name is for the woman who looks after us."

While they walked back to the hall, Heidi and Cairenn talked ceaselessly about what had transpired since they last saw each other.

Egill told Tor about his work repairing ships instead of rowing them. No word had come back yet regarding Bjarni's voyage to Vinland. People were speculating that Skræling ate Bjarni and all his men. Tor prayed that this summer would bring news.

Egill and Cairenn had gotten passage on the knorr owned by Thorstan Hrolfger of Brattahlid. "Thorimm Hrolfgersson told me to tell you that the Skræling woman would not be welcomed back in Brattahlid. His family owns the ship we came on. In fact, he, or rather his father, owns the shop I work in. He wanted me to deliver this message," Egill said nervously.

"It matters not, we go where we like. We have power too and do not quiver in front of some sniveling son of a supposed lord. We cannot allow unjust laws to stand, nor can we allow unjust men enforce those unjust laws," Tor said nonchalantly. "I think we have a lamb ready for the pot, do we not, Heidi?"

Two days after Egill and Cairenn arrived in Iceland, Heidi went into labor. Cairenn volunteered to serve as midwife and took charge. Heidi had informed her that she knew she was carrying two little ones and was anticipating a long and difficult delivery. She called on another woman from Borg to help Cairenn with the birth when the time came.

Heidi went through her normal energy spurt early that morning, but when she squatted to milk the two cows, her water broke, she lost her balance and plopped onto her back beside the gentle brown cow.

Cairenn was up and was just getting started with milking the goats. Cairenn raised the alarm and soon Heidi was in her birthing bed with Cairenn attending to her while Egill and Tor were rushing to town to fetch Ingris Louderfulmerswife to help deliver the babies. Before the sun went low in the western sky, Heidi held a new daughter at each breast.

One was born with a thick shock of black hair, light-colored eyes, and pink skin. The second child had only a few wisps of light-colored hair, almost black eyes, and darker-colored skin. Tor insisted they be named Bjarta Stjarna, Bright Star and Heidr Tungl, Bright Moon. Heidi was reluctant to give a daughter her own name, but finally acquiesced. Taking it further, Heidi argued that all her children should have Norse names to lessen their chance of being harassed due to their heritage.

Now it was Tor's turn to acquiesce. *Bjarta Stjarna* was given Tor's mother's namesake, Erna, while Heidr Tungl was given Tor's grandmother's name, Gerdis. They would use the Monongahela names only within the family. Tor was uncomfortable making these concessions, but Heidi convinced him that they knew before they left Turtle Island that life would be hard for her. She willingly accepted those hardships to be at his side and would have it no other way. Giving her children Norse names was a small price for the children's future safety and happiness.

———

HEIDI AND CAIRENN conspired to convince Egill to stay in Iceland and work on the farm. Tor sent a small bag of silver coins to Hryn, in Greenland, on the ship that Egill and Cairenn were to sail on. The gesture was intended to allow Hryn to hire a new housemaid.

Tor and Egill worked well together, and the farm prospered, soon becoming the largest sheep farm in western Iceland. Tor's reputation as a fair and honest businessman producing fine wool and valuable sheep spread far and wide in western Iceland. Unknown to Tor, that was causing him a problem.

———

Ferrminn Homallarsson had inherited the former largest sheep ranch in western Greenland. Ferrminn had developed a strong like for ale and spent much of his time in the alehouse in Borg bragging about his great farm and famous wool to all the sailors who came into the establishment when they were in port. The problem was, he was not doing his part to maintain the great farm his ancestors had built. The farm was in decline, and Ferrminn concluded that was mostly Tor Eriksson's fault. Furthermore, Tor had a Skræling whore for a wife, and should not be allowed to be a landholder at all.

A LOOK AT BOOK SIX

ICELAND

In a land of stark beauty, one family's resilience will shape the course of generations.

For Tor and Heidi, settling in Iceland was meant to be a fresh start. But hostility toward Heidi's Skraeling heritage—and her children—tests their dreams of building a prosperous life.

Defying the odds, they forge alliances and defend their farm against violent attacks. Yet their struggle for acceptance continues. Tor must navigate Iceland's intricate legal system to protect his family, while Heidi faces every parent's nightmare when two of her children are abducted. Their desperate pursuit across the rugged wilderness pushes them to their limits and strengthens their bond in unexpected ways.

As old enemies resurface and challenges persist, Tor and Heidi's determination to leave a lasting legacy carries on through their children—and their children's children—etched into Icelandic history.

Embark on a powerful saga of love, sacrifice, and enduring hope as one family fights to claim their place in an unforgiving world.

AVAILABLE FEBRUARY 2025

ABOUT THE AUTHOR

Ron Briggs is a veteran, having served four years in the USAF. His education includes a Bachelor of Science in Range and Wildlife Ecology at Oklahoma State University and a Master of Science in Range and Wildlife Management at Texas A&I University.

He is retired from the USDA-Natural Resources Conservation Service, and his career encompassed twenty-five years as District Conservationist in Linn County, Kansas. Prior to college, he worked seven years in the building trades.

Having developed a deep interest in history, especially in the pre-colonial period of North America, Ron's interests prompted him to begin researching a pre-history story about the Tallgrass Prairie Region of the Great Plains. That research evolved into his current multi-volume work, the Yellow Hair series, which includes scenes from northern Europe to the mountains of western North America.

Ron and his wife, Debbie, currently live in Mound City, Kansas, and have two grown children and seven grandchildren. His interests include spending time with family, writing, hunting, fishing, traveling, and woodworking.

BIBLIOGRAPHY

Appelt, Martin. "Man, Culture and Environment in Ancient Greenland." Publication No. 4, Danish Polar Center.

Bierhorst, John . *Mythology of the Lanape: Guide and Texts.* University of Arizona Press, 1995.

Bronsted, Johannes. *The Vikings.* Penguin Books, London, 1960, Revised 1965.

Clarke, Helen and Bjorn Ambrosiani. *Towns in the Viking Age.* St. Martin's Press, New York, 1995.

Cohat, Yves, tr. Ruth Daniel, Ruth. *The Vikings: Lords of the Seas.* Gallimard, 1987.

Damas, David. *Arctic, Vol. 5, Handbook of North American Indians.* Smithsonian Press, Washington, D.C., 1984.

Charles River Editors. *Native American Tribes: The History and Culture of the Inuit (Eskimos).*

Feasel, Charles T. *White Bear.* Ballantine Books, New York, 1990.

Fitzhugh, William and Elizabeth Ward. *Vikings, The North Atlantic Saga.* Smithsonian Press, Washington, D.C., 2000.

Gordon,E. V., rev by A. R. Taylor. *An Introduction to Old Norse.* Oxford Press, London.

Gronnow, Bjarn. *Late Dorset in High Arctic Greenland: Final Report on the Gateway to Greenland Project.* Canadian Archeological Association, 1999.

Grumet, Robert S. *The Lenapes (Indians of North America).* Chelsea House Publishing, 1989.

Harrington, Mark R. *Religion and Ceremonies of the Lenape.* Forgotten Books, 2012.

Harrington, Mark R. *The Indians of New Jersey, Dickon Among the Lanapes.* Rutgers University Press, New Jersey, 1966.

Heckewelder, John Gotlieb Ernestus, notes by William C. Reichel.*History, Manners, and Customs of The Indian Nations*

Who Inhabited Pennsylvania and the Neighbouring States. Historical Society of Pennsylvania, 1881.

Ingstad, Anne Stine et al. .*The Discovery of a Norse Settlement in America. Excavations at L'Anse aux Meadows, Newfoundland, 1961-1968.* =Tromso, 1977.

Jones, Gwynne. *A History of the Vikings*. Oxford University Press, 1968, 1973, 1984.

Kunz, Keneva, tr., edited by Gisli Sigurdsson. *The Vinland Sagas*. Penguin Books, London, 2008.

McCullough, K. M. "The Ruin Islanders: Thule Culture Pioneers in the High Eastern Arctic." Archeological Survey of Canada, 141, Canadian Museum of Civilization, 1989.

McGee, Robert. *Ancient People of the Arctic*. University of British Columbia Press, Vancouver, 1996.

McGee, Robert. *The Last Imaginary Place*. Oxford University Press, New York, 2005.

Mcleod, William Christi. "The Family Hunting Territory and Lenape Political Organization." American Anthropology 24.

Maschner, Herbert, Owen Masson Owen, and Robert McGee. *The Northern World AD 900-1400*. The University of Utah Press, Salt Lake City, 2009.

Maxwell, Moreau S. *Prehistory of the Eastern Arctic*. Academic Press, New York, 1985.

Means, Bernard K. *Circular Villages of the Monongahela Tradition*. The University of Alabama Press, Tuscaloosa, 2007.

Rasmusen, Knud. *Eskimo Folk Tales*. Gyldendal, Copenhagen, 1921.

Roesdahl, Else. *The Vikings*. Penguin Books, New York, 1987.

Schledermann, Peter. *Crossroads to Greenland, 3000 Years of Prehistory in the Eastern High Arctic.* The Arctic Institute of North America of the University of Calgary, 1990.

Seaver, Kirsten A. The Frozen Echo, Greenland and the Exploration of North America, ca. A.D. 1000-1500. Stanford University Press, Stanford, CA, 1996.

Simpson, Jacqueline. *Everyday Life in the Viking Age.* Dorset Press, New York, 1967.

Sutherland, Patricia, ed. *Contributions to the Study of Dorset Paleo Eskimos.* Canada Museum of History, 2005.

Trigger, Bruce G. *Northeast, Vol 15, Handbook of North American Indians.* Smithsonian Institution Press, Washington, D.C., 1984.

Weslager, C. A. *The Delaware Indians: A History.* Rutgers University Press, New Jersey, 1972.